THE BUR'

JOHN FRANCIS HART

A tale of the struggle by two sisters

to become medically qualified

set against Victorian prejudice.

To Winefride

1

'I have just one daughter but, by heaven, I would rather follow her coffin to the grave than allow her to get involved in such a thing.'

'That's a bit strong, James.'

'I mean it. The whole idea is revolting. I would really prefer not even to think about it. It is not something a respectable woman would even contemplate.'

James, like his lunch companions, was one of the Academicals, a term used, not always affectionately by other members of the Regency Club, to describe the small group who had all attended the City Academy around the start of the reign of Victoria and had remained in close friendship and with closed minds in the forty years since. Their Wednesday lunch at the Club followed by brandies in the Members' Lounge was a ritual. Woe betide any other member who was sufficiently ill-advised to occupy one of their preferred leather easy chairs beside the fire.

James was a lawyer whose neck had expanded along with his practice to make enormous demands on his collar, especially when he was incensed as now, when pressed by his accountant friend Alistair, for his views on women doctors. Alistair, as befitted a man who dealt strictly in numbers, was spare like his columns of figures and had a slightly malicious habit of goading his friends to see their reactions. He stroked his cheek with a long bony forefinger.

'Well you may have to think about it, James, because of what that woman has started. What about you, George? You're a medical man. What do you think? Or are you too worried that they will start to take business away from you?'

George smiled a little sardonically, secure in being unchallengeable in all things medical. 'The matter is quite simple. I don't go as far as James but there is ample scientific evidence that women have smaller brains than men and are quite incapable of coping with the hard, incessant study which is involved in medical training. And certainly, they could not deal with the great responsibility that is part of medical, far less surgical practice.'

Alistair curled his lips sarcastically. 'Oh, come off it, George. My memory of you and your fellow medics at University is that the only hard and incessant study was carried out in the drinking shops down the Vennel. But you're quite right. When you think of the huge developments in medicine and science over the past years by people like Lister and Faraday and - saving your presence, William- Charles Darwin, I am not aware of any contribution whatsoever made by any member of the fair sex. And that speaks for itself.'

William, who had risen from an unlikely start to become Professor of Divinity at the University bestirred himself from his post-lunch drowsiness at the mention of Darwin but decided not to rise to the bait. The firelight reflected on his round, bald head as he spoke. 'I will agree, James, on one thing. My good lady is very caring and like all of our wives does lots of charitable work, but could you imagine consulting one of them on something serious?'

There was a pause while they all mentally rejected the idea as fatuous. They were the only members still in the Long Room whose tall windows overlooked Regency Square where it was already starting to get dark. The only sound from outside was the noise of carriage wheels and horses' hooves. Then William said,

'Who was that woman, James– Fotherindale? – Remember, she was much in the news after the war in the Crimea.'

'Florence Nightingale. But I think she herself said that women make first class nurses but would make second rate doctors. And even then, the role of nurse is more suited to women of the lower classes. It is totally unsuited to ladies who have been brought up in a much more refined background. As you say, William, our good ladies already do fine work in the various charitable activities in which they are involved. They would understandably shrink from any closer contact with persons who are strangers to them and to their class.'

Alistair smirked. 'And I was just joking, George, about women setting up in competition with you. Who in their right mind would consult a woman doctor? I wouldn't, and I certainly would not permit my wife to do so. Another round of drinks, men?'

George ordered another round of brandies and while they were awaiting their arrival asked, 'What started all this talk, Alistair?'

'I was telling James about that chap, Burton. You know the chap. He's from Newcastle or around there. Made a fortune in shipping. He's been a member for a couple of years, but I don't know if he fits in. He's just not one of us, if you know what I mean.'

'You don't mean he's Jewish.'

'Good Lord no,' said Alistair, 'Although I shouldn't be surprised if there were something there in the background if you dug back a little. Like that man, Montrose, you remember, William? You thought he must have some connection with Graham of Claverhouse and it turned out he had merely changed his name from Rosenberg. No. Burton's just an awkward sort of cove. Remember the fuss he made when the Club Steward was sacked? All that nonsense about the man's rights. Anyway, the thing is that his two daughters have both enrolled in that woman's establishment to study medicine. I don't really know him, but my wife calls on his wife and I can tell you that the lady is in a state of shock about the whole thing.'

William was still puzzled. 'Who is "that woman", as you call her?'

'You must know her. Her name is Miss Clegg. Jennifer Clegg. She is tall and severe and always wears black - possibly always the same gown - and she strides about the town with great mannish steps. She is always accompanied by a lady she calls her Secretary who is small and has almost to run to keep up. I was in the Senate when she sought permission to open her establishment and I can tell you that she is formidable; not a hint of woman about her. She demanded rather than asked for permission. I, of course, voted against but you know how some of those University men like to see themselves as keeping up with the times. At least that is how they expressed it.'

James, with the air of one used to having his views unchallenged, interjected from the depths of his armchair 'If keeping up with the times means discarding the standards which have guided our civilisation to what we can pride ourselves is its present level of excellence then I prefer to keep what we have.'

To this his acolytes nodded their approval.

'And I repeat that I would rather follow my dear daughter's bier to the grave than have her do something so far beneath her. What was that fellow Burton thinking of?'

2

That fellow Burton had been doing a great deal of thinking. He had come to the city from the North of England where, starting with nothing, he had worked his way up in shipbuilding to his present position as owner of a prosperous shipping line. From the beginning, he was obsessed with efficiency, which made him stand out for completing every task with the most effective use of time and materials.

He also, at an early age, developed a critical sense, which made him scrutinise everything no matter how longstanding its general acceptance. It was this that made him doubt the industry's continued dependence on sail for trading ships and made him reach the conclusion, ahead of nearly everyone else, that the future lay in steam and steel. In pursuing this he had the support of a Scottish engineer, John MacGregor, called inevitably, Mac, with whom he worked for thirty-five years without any written agreement between them. They were never friends, but Burton knew that in a crisis there was no better man to have at his side. At the outset, their business had, on a number of occasions, sailed close to the wind (or perhaps better metaphorically to say, come near to running out of coal) but they had pulled through and made their fortune.

Burton was above medium height with receding black hair and clean shaven in an era when most men wore beards. (It is possible to speculate that had the fashion been for clean shaven he would have sported a beard). He was powerfully built, with a working man's hands. When he was working in the shipyards he carried an air of suppressed violence that bullied people into submission even though he had not actually struck anyone since he was an apprentice. He had, however, learnt to play the polished drawing room charmer and treated ladies with an almost exaggerated courtesy as if they were butterflies which he was afraid he might crush. It was this combination of power and gentleness that drew his wife to him.

The only major blow he had suffered was the loss of his only son in infancy. That was something from which he could never fully recover. The gaping void would never disappear, but he had disciplined himself to skirt around it. But to balance the books as it were (which was the way his mind through force of habit worked) his wife had subsequently given birth to two daughters, now in their early twenties, of whom he was inordinately proud. Unusually, it was he rather than his wife who was most involved in shaping their characters, almost as if he was devoting to them the education he would have given to his son.

Fortunately for them, the girls had taken their looks principally from their mother. Alice, the elder, was tall and dark and she had an air of unflurried calm about her which showed itself in the way she talked and walked and conducted herself. Caroline was slightly smaller although of good height, with a fairer complexion and she walked, as she did everything else, briskly. Alice, without giving much thought to the matter, dressed almost entirely as her mother would have wished; Caroline, with as little effort, chose clothes that displeased her. From a very early age her impetuosity had got her into scrapes from which Alice, as the elder sister, had to rescue her. Impetuosity involves a lack of foresight, including a reckless disregard of other people's feelings and Caroline was slow to realise that. But Mr Burton saw in Caroline something of himself and this made him overlook perhaps more that he should.

One Sunday afternoon Mr Burton was relaxing in his house, a very large stone-built mansion with extensive grounds in the best part of the city. He was in his study, unusually for him not toiling at his business affairs but taking a moment of leisure to do some reading. The study reflected the man. It was a working room. There were very few books and those that were there, were of a scientific or engineering character. There were no paintings; instead the room was decorated with draughtsmen's drawings of ships in various stages of construction accompanied by scale models of the completed vessels. One of the few exceptions to the general paucity of books was the one that George Burton was currently reading, Palgrave's Golden Treasury. Inexplicably, this great bull of a man loved poetry, a passion he kept strictly to himself. Some years previously he had found himself on a long sea voyage to India and, as this was the only book to be found on board, he had forced himself to overcome an initial reluctance and he had read and re-read it, until eventually what had been a discipline became a joy.

He was, therefore, in a peaceful frame of mind when there was a knock at the door and he slid the book into his desk drawer as both of his daughters came in. Alice began to speak but, to her annoyance, before she could finish asking whether her father was enjoying the spring weather, Caroline burst out,

'Papa we want to study to become doctors.'

Mr Burton was bewildered. 'Alice, what on earth is your sister talking about?'

Alice began to explain about Miss Clegg and how she was planning to open a College where ladies could train to be doctors but before she could finish Mr Burton, who was becoming increasingly angry as she spoke, interrupted her by rising and, as he often did when he was perturbed, paced up and down with his hands joined behind his back.

'That woman you mention, Miss Clegg. 'Doctor', she calls herself although heaven only knows how she came by that title. I have little knowledge of her, but I do know that she has given great offence to some people of high standing in the medical world.' He turned. 'You would degrade yourselves hopelessly by such a course. I am deeply hurt, no, not hurt, disgusted, by what you propose. There is a place for women of a lower class to minister to the sick, say, in a nursing position, but these are women who, through their background have perforce come into contact with a side of life from which thankfully you have been spared. But to think that my daughters - ' He broke off. He preferred *not* to think of his daughters in that way.

Alice tried to speak but Burton waved her down. 'Become doctors? Preposterous. Have you taken leave of your senses? The whole matter is out of the question. The answer is no and that is final. I don't want to hear another word. Please be good enough to leave my study.'

Caroline was about to say something, but Alice restrained her with a gesture and the two girls left the study with their heads down. Carefully avoiding meeting their mother, whom Alice was concerned might have heard raised voices from the study, they made their way upstairs to Alice's bedroom. After Alice had closed the door she turned to Caroline, who quailed to see her usually calm sister flushed with anger. Alice normally gave an impression of serenity, which was indeed natural to her, but underneath there was a suppressed fury that, when it surfaced, made her as fearsome as her father. One or two of the house servants had found this out to their cost.

'Caroline, Caroline. Why did you do it? You agreed that you would keep absolutely quiet and let me broach the subject with Papa, but I had barely opened my mouth when you barged in and ruined everything.'

This time Caroline had the sense to say nothing in her own defence (she knew there was no defence) and she watched as Alice paced up and down.

Alice had carefully prepared the approach she was going to make to their father. He had developed the habit of discussing with her the business decisions he was contemplating. From this she had unconsciously picked up some of the ways by which he was able to persuade people to his way of thinking. In particular, at the outset of a negotiation, he would propose something totally outrageous and then, having put this extreme thought in the minds of his adversaries, he allowed them to persuade him to accept a lower position - the one he had in mind all along. The trouble was that in Alice's case the extreme result was the very one she wanted to obtain from the start and she could not think of a more extreme position from which to retire. At one time, she had talked generally with her father about the Oxford Movement which some years previously had shaken the Church in England and she had toyed with the idea of announcing that she was going to become a Roman Catholic nun and using that as her opening. But she realised that even that, horrible as it was, would pale into insignificance in her father's mind beside the thought of her becoming a doctor.

So, that wouldn't work. She had thought her way carefully through other ideas and the final strategy she plumped for, after much discussion with Caroline (whose wilder notions she used as a prod to her own thinking) was to adopt a softly, softly approach to make her father accustomed to the idea, bit by bit. The discussion today was supposed to have been the first step, What a disaster.

Caroline, sitting on the bed, at last spoke, unusually for her, hesitantly and without looking at her sister. 'I... I am so sorry, Alice.'

Alice stopped pacing and turned to look at her. 'Is that it? Is it all over?' she said. 'It was you who first came up with this idea of becoming a doctor and who persuaded me. Is that all to be abandoned?'

Poor Caroline was still so shaken by the scene with her father and her own part in causing it that she had no thought for what might happen next. Her present misery filled all her thoughts and she had difficulty in grasping what Alice was saying. Through her tears, she asked Alice what she meant.

'I had not thought of becoming a doctor until you put the idea into my head. But it is firmly there now. I realised that the way I was brought up by Papa, my love of learning, my desire to help those in trouble, all these things combined in convincing me that my calling in life was to be a doctor. Nothing has changed that, and nothing will.' She paused. 'But that doesn't mean that you have to tag along.'

Caroline jumped up. The phrase 'tag along' riled her. 'Not at all, Alice. It was I who first wished to be a doctor and it was you who followed me. I was so upset by what has just happened and the way my foolishness had caused it that I could think of nothing else. But I want to go on. And to go on even if you don't.'

This last was said quite forcibly but Alice was used to her sister and did not take offence. She hugged Caroline, and they sat side by side on the bed as Alice set out her plan to advance even more carefully; it had to be done by her alone. Caroline's sole role was to express her sorrow to her father for the distress she caused him and thereafter to avoid totally any reference to their future plans. After what had happened Alice was confident that Caroline would stick with this decision.

3

Caroline duly made her peace with her father and, as promised, thereafter kept out of the way, although she was irked, because for some time absolutely nothing seemed to be happening. Her father and Alice talked quite amicably about the sort of things they normally discussed; Mr Burton came and went to his office, but Alice never seemed to be seeking the head–to-head meeting Caroline thought necessary and which she tried to facilitate by making herself scarce as much as possible. So much so that her father asked whether she was feeling quite well. Caroline was quite well, at least as well as someone could be, who was so consumed with anxiety and impatience - especially impatience. Alice reassured her that everything was going according to her plan, but Caroline was not reassured and often lay awake at night turning over in her mind outlandish schemes, one of which she might adopt if the attempt failed. If her parents had had any inkling of these nocturnal thoughts, they themselves would have had little sleep but fortunately night-time plans quickly fade away in the cold light of day.

Alice bided her time, confident that if she were patient, something would happen to give her the chance to re-open the matter. She made sure that she was bright when her father came home from business and discussed with him the books she was reading. He always took an interest as, without wishing to read them himself, he made it his business to know what books were beneficial for her. Alice even tried to distract her mother from intruding too much on her father's quiet time, as she was aware, although it was never mentioned, that sometimes her father was a little irritated by her mother's wish to press upon him the social gossip of their acquaintances (and 'acquaintance' is an elastic term in the realm of gossip) an interest which he did not share. Mr Burton had no real interest in people; only in what they did or might do. While for Mrs Burton, gossip reflected genuine interest and concern for other's welfare, perhaps extending too widely.

One day, when Alice and her father were discussing Melville's Moby Dick in which he, as a seafaring man, took a special interest, he told her how pleased he was that she and Caroline had shown such an aptitude in reading and following his guidance in developing their minds. He said how proud he was when she and Caroline had taken it on themselves the previous year to take on the work to obtain the Certificate of Education and not only that, but had come out with the highest marks.

Alice, in thanking him, told him that she and her sister owed everything to him. She said quietly that they felt they were trying to fill the gap that the death of their brother in infancy had left. Mr Burton tried not to show how moved he was by what she had said. He merely patted her hand as she sat beside him.

Alice then turned to him. 'Papa, do you know why we decided to sit the exams?'

'I suppose to prove to yourselves the level of your scholarship.'

'No, Papa. Caroline and I didn't need exams to satisfy that.'

She looked him straight in the face and reached out to hold his hand looking at him steadfastly all the time she was speaking. 'Caroline and I took the exams because it was a necessary preliminary to our taking up the study of medicine.'

Mr Burton looked at her in incredulity, but he did not remove his hand from hers. There was a long silence. If Caroline had been there she would have been unable to keep quiet. But Alice, either through intuition or because her father had taught her, said nothing to break the silence, which went on and on.

Eventually Mr Burton rose and paced up and down in his habitual way. When he turned, Alice realised he had a tear in his eye.

'I said a few moments ago that I was proud of you and your sister. I am even more proud now. When you raised the matter before, I spoke impulsively and harshly. I talked of the terrible consequences of doing what you wanted to do, both social and personal. I did not give you and your sister the credit that you would have already thought of these things and made the decision that you wanted to proceed, despite all the dreadful drawbacks - and they are dreadful much more than you anticipate. That takes resolve and courage. We Burtons don't follow the herd. I have often said if a thing is unpopular it is probably right. And by heaven this would be unpopular.' He resumed his pacing up and down with Alice watching every movement before he turned to her again. 'I will support you in what you want to do.'

He held up his hand as she tried to speak. 'No, don't interrupt. There is only one stipulation. If you ever take up a medical position you will accept no payment and I will compensate you accordingly. It is bad enough to embark on this way of life but to accept recompense for it would be beneath your station. I will support you, but I will not give you my blessing. I feel too much that it is a wrong decision. However, I have brought you up to make decisions on your own and so be it.'

Alice rose slowly. She had no words. She looked at her father and then crossed over to where he stood and threw her arms around him in a way she had not done since she was a child. Mr Burton, always so unbending, for a second did not react and then pressed her close to him.

'My dear, dear child. Now off you go and tell your sister. But keep it to yourselves. I will have to give thought to what we are going to tell your mother.'

4

Alice could not know it, but she had chosen an ideal time to renew her efforts. Her father had reacted violently to the original approach but, although he had told his daughters to put the whole idea totally out of their minds, he himself did not find it so easy to forget it. Despite his best efforts, he found himself returning to it time after time, but always internally. He was very fond of his wife and they lived together very amicably, each operating in their respective spheres with only occasional disputes when the spheres collided (disputes which were always resolved to Mr Burton's satisfaction) but he had never thought to involve his wife in discussions on important matters and did not think to do so now.

He had many business acquaintances, but no friends. When the family had come to live in the town they had been made most welcome and many had sought to know him in view of his business success. But he never felt totally at home in any of the informal social groups which made up male society in the city, where a family connection, however vague, was sufficient to give an immediate entrée to activities from which he seemed to be omitted. He felt himself to be an outsider and when a person has that feeling he behaves awkwardly; in contrast to another person who fits seamlessly in. Accordingly, he had no intimates to confide in, but, as he did in business, he kept alert for any talk which might show how people were thinking.

There was one person in particular whom Mr Burton tried to avoid, as he regarded him as a buffoon, but, as is the way of things, this man, Carmichael, sought his company whenever he could, possibly because Carmichael instinctively thought that this outsider would have time for him. Whenever they met, Mr Burton made no attempt to hide his dislike, or more truthfully his contempt and he was unconcerned at any hurt which the other might suffer. Carmichael, for his part, hated each rebuff and the man who gave it, but he could not help still trying to seek his favour.

A few weeks after his daughters' original approach to him, Mr Burton met Carmichael as he was walking down the Broadwalk. He nodded in acknowledgement and made to hurry on, but Carmichael was not to be put off and when Mr Burton, in response to his query, told him where he was going he offered to accompany him, as he was going the same way.

Carmichael burbled on without Mr Burton paying much heed to what he was saying. Then he mentioned the name Clegg and that immediately gained Mr Burton's attention. Carmichael had heard that Miss Clegg, whom Carmichael seemed to regard as a figure of fun, had received permission to open her college for the training of lady doctors. Carmichael then proceeded to trot out the very arguments which Mr Burton had been revolving in his mind as to why this idea was ludicrous. He finished by saying that the venture was bound to fail as no lady would wish to be involved, knowing that by doing so she would rightly forfeit her position in society.

Mr Burton eventually shook off Carmichael with an even greater abruptness than usual and strode off, but instead of turning towards his intended destination he kept straight on, his mind in a whirl of competing thoughts. That fool, who had never had an original thought in his head, was babbling the very objections which Mr Burton had voiced. But if Carmichael was saying these things without any thought at all was it possible that he himself was doing the same and like a parrot repeating opinions he had not considered properly? Certainly, the idea that women did not have the mental capacity to study medicine was manifest nonsense as he knew from the results of his daughters' performance in their examinations. And if that was a nonsense what about the other objections? Try as he might he could not clear his mind as he went along. Only one thing was sure; his anger that a buffoon like Carmichael would dare to suggest that his daughters, if they did what they wanted, would become pariahs in society. The consequence of all this was that Alice, when she renewed her approach, was able to get to her father through a door which was already ajar.

Things were very different where Mrs Burton was concerned. She and her friend, Mrs Jamieson, shared a common view on nearly everything of importance. They thought their near neighbour, Mrs Hope, dressed most inappropriately given the fact that it was less than two years since the death of her husband; they were horrified at the way that Mrs Jamieson's young cousin had married far beneath her; they thought it even more wrong that the daughter of another friend had recently been seen frequently in the company of the son of Lord Millfield. 'Surely', said Mrs Jamieson 'she realises that she is totally outwith her station in life. People recognise that. They will think of her as an upstart and she will lose all dignity and position.'

Mrs Burton could only nod in agreement with this before turning her attention to the matter which was uppermost in both their minds: the Jamiesons' elder son, Edward. He was just a few years older than Alice and both mothers, for some time now, had regarded this as an ideal match. Unfortunately, while Alice had a slim dark attractiveness, she had no real interest in the parties and balls which her mother thought should be the major preoccupation of a young lady of her age. Alice had, perhaps, spent too much time with her father to regard young men of her own age as anything but shallow and silly. To some extent her perception was self fulfilling; many a young man had approached her with the type of light-hearted chatter which, given a more receptive audience, might have developed into something genuinely witty. However, before Alice's steady gaze the prospective suitor would feel his confidence draining and he would degenerate into babble that even he recognised as mindless, before making his escape to less taxing company.

Neither her mother nor Mrs Jamieson regarded this as a major difficulty. They had lately been discussing a suitable place for the young couple to live and had decided on the Rowanhill area of the city where the houses were admittedly not so grand as the Burtons' existing mansion but still an ideal place for a young couple to start off married life together.

They had not devoted the same amount of thought to Caroline's future. She was of course younger but, in Mrs Burton's view, she was in any event a Father's girl brought up as a tomboy - at least mentally - and Mrs Burton did not have the same empathy with her as she did with Alice. She rather expected that Caroline would marry someone of whom she did not approve, but that was the worst of her imaginings

Thus, as she and her husband were together one Sunday afternoon after their mid-day meal, her thoughts were very far from those exercising the other members of her family. And it is little wonder that her thoughts were centred on purely domestic matters. If Mr Burton had considered it at all, he would have put down his daughters' undoubted intellectual abilities to his background and his training. His wife had, from time to time, chided him for bringing up the girls in what seemed to her to be a masculine way. And in truth, if she had been asked to what the girls owed their intelligence, she, being pre-conditioned to discount her own bright mind and abilities, would have agreed with her husband. Mrs Burton's considerable musical abilities, for example, had been curbed to fall in with the very limited musical tastes of her husband and her other interests had been stunted not necessarily by him but also by her earlier upbringing. Just as the feet of Japanese women of class were rumoured to be bound, to restrict their size to what was regarded as fashionable for a lady, so she had been moulded to fit what was regarded as right. Her daughters' development had not been so restricted. Mrs Burton would come to regret it had not.

'Mr Burton, my dear, do stop pacing up and down. Sit down and read your newspaper.'

Mr Burton did not sit down but he stood still and said, 'Alice wants to become a doctor. So, does Caroline.'

Mrs Burton was not sure if she was supposed to say anything in return. It was like saying 'Alice wants to go to the moon.' Husbands and wives often say things to each other which slip through the other's consciousness without leaving a mark or requiring a response. She smiled benignly at her husband and let her mind slip back to her reverie of house hunting for Alice, before realising that she was being looked at for a more positive response.

'I'm sorry my dear. You said?'

'Alice and Caroline want to become doctors'

'I don't understand.'

Mr Burton repeated patiently. 'Alice and Caroline want to go and study and work at a hospital and become doctors.'

Mrs Burton was still lost. In her experience, young ladies did not work to become anything except getting married. She didn't know how to frame a response because she didn't know what information she required. 'You mean...'

'There is a lady in the city, a Miss Jennifer Clegg, who apparently is a qualified medical person, and she is starting a college in town to train other ladies to become doctors. Alice and Caroline wish to attend.'

At this point, Alice and Caroline, themselves, returned from their afternoon walk and came in to join their parents. Mrs Burton looked at them almost uncomprehendingly before turning her attention back to her husband. Even then, so extreme was the proposition, that it took nearly half an hour of patient repetition by Mr Burton and not so patient interjections from Caroline (despite her sister's disapproval) before she fully grasped what was intended. And she was aghast. Somewhat to Mr Burton's irritation she had always accepted his word as law, but so horrified was she, that she protested more vehemently than ever before in her married life (and indeed ever after). The immediate blow was to the marriage plans so carefully drawn up. These had not yet been shared with Mr Burton (or, for that matter, Alice) but, in an area in which Mrs Burton devoted such interest, she had little doubt that he would fall in with her wishes. That alone would have caused her enormous grief. But to become a doctor!

'How could you even countenance such a thing, Mr Burton. It is completely out of the question.'

Mr Burton, for the first time in his married life under attack by his wife, could only reply that it was indeed the question. Alice managed to keep Caroline from intervening and spoke at length to her mother setting out their plans and their dreams. To no avail.

'Have you no thought to your daughters' futures? They will be putting themselves totally outwith society. Who will marry them if they embark on such a thing?' And poor Mrs Burton's tears overwhelmed her, as they did on numerous future occasions on which the matter was raised. She rushed from the room, followed by

Alice, who gave such succour as she could, given that she was herself partly to blame for her mother's distress.

Discussions continued for some days. But, while these discussions seemed full, Mr Burton and his wife each had misgivings they felt unable to share with the other. Mr Burton, in his younger days, had come across many men studying to become doctors and in a student body in which bad behaviour was rather expected, the medical students (outdone only by the divinity students) stood out for their rowdyism, licentiousness and brutality. The change when they qualified was extraordinary but, until then, no decent girl would have retained her reputation for a second in their collective company.

For Mrs Burton, lying awake in the night, the horrors grew unabated. She could not bring herself to discuss with her husband the sights which, in the course of his profession, a doctor must see, and which were totally unsuited to the eyes of a young lady. When she married, Mrs Burton had come to her wedding night totally unprepared by her own mother for what was to happen, and, despite her husband's care, the whole process had remained something to be endured and certainly not discussed. In her whole married life, she had never seen her husband naked, nor he her. When Alice came to puberty Mrs Burton had no choice but to deal with her menstrual bleeding, but explained it as a fact of female life, without relating it to reproduction. Alice was astonished to know that her mother had suffered this monthly pain without Alice being aware of it, but her mother brushed aside any further reference to it, leaving Alice to explain things as best she could to Caroline when her turn came. Mrs Burton was, however, able to discuss with her daughters the natural development of their breasts, and even the advent of underarm hair, as dealing with this was regarded by Mrs Burton as part of feminine grooming. There was, of course, never any mention of anything below the waistline.

Now her daughters were to be exposed to the very things which polite society did not acknowledge to take place. Almost to feed her horror she would allow herself to imagine something of what might be involved... only to turn away with renewed disgust. What made it worse was that not only would her daughters be exposed to such sights, but other people would know they had seen them. It would taint them irretrievably.

The discussions continued for some time without conclusion, although they were nearly derailed by Caroline declaring at one stage that she was going, willy nilly. It took all Alice's diplomacy to get things back on course. For his part, Mr Burton, in his business dealings, once he had made a decision was accustomed to put it into effect without delay but he was here faced with the unprecedented outspoken opposition of his wife. Normally this would not have affected him, but he knew that by granting the girls the permission they sought he would cause his wife not just displeasure but real sorrow, almost despair. And despite the way he often acted he was not an unkind man. But the girls' ambitions...

Finally, one day, Mr Burton gathered everyone in the drawing room and said he had made his decision. He had paid the fees for the required four years' tuition and the girls should be allowed to take their places.

Mrs Burton took to her bed.

5

By the time the first day at the medical school came, Mrs Burton was still not seeing visitors. However, she was sufficiently recovered to rise from her bed to take part in the only aspect of the proceedings over which she had any control, the choosing of the appropriate outfits for the girls' first day of medical training. The matter was complicated by Alice's insistence, to her mother's horror, that they would travel to their place of study not, as their father wished, using the family carriage, but, as a sign of their new independent life, by means of the horse drawn tram which ran on rails recently extended close to their house. This news – and the thought of her friends' reactions - was almost enough to send Mrs Burton to seek refuge back in her room at the thought of her friends' reaction, but the necessity of making sure that nothing worse happened was sufficient to hold her to the task.

The discussions involved not only the two girls and their mother but also Anna, one of the servants, who acted as a ladies' maid for the sisters. 'Ladies' Maid' may have been Anna's official position but she was much more than that to the girls. Anna, slim and neat both in her dress and in her manner, was their supporter and confidante, a constant calming presence for them, especially in curbing Caroline's high spirits, although she and Caroline were much of an age. She was. Alice depended on her but, in the way of bookish people, was somehow more interested in her fictional characters than the actual people she met. Caroline, on the other hand, was always interested in what people did and knew the background of all the servants. But, despite her probing, she could discover nothing of Anna's private life as Anna smilingly deflected all Caroline's subtle (subtle at least in Caroline's eyes) queries as to her circumstances away from the Burton household.'

Thus, the views on appropriate dresses ranged from Mrs Burton's proposal of something which might have been fitting for a tea party, down to Caroline's more utilitarian ideas, involving her at one stage bemoaning the fact that they were not able, like men, to wear sensible clothes like trousers. Mrs Burton threw up her hands at this and a row could have developed but Anna intervened to calm the waters and eventually obtained general agreement on walking out dresses of fairly sombre hue.

Mrs Burton was still dismayed by the thought of the girls being seen boarding a public conveyance and she insisted that Anna should accompany them down the hill to the tram stop. As this was the first time they had gone on a tram they were, despite their apparent nonchalance, a little unsure of themselves but Alice led the way on board. As they made their way along the tram a large young man stumbled to his feet and startled Caroline by speaking to her, although she could not make out what he was saying. When she raised her eyebrows, he flushed and repeated what he had said. This time Caroline grasped that he was offering her his seat but some imp in her made her affect that she still did not understand. It forced him to repeat his offer, although he was by this time so flustered and red that, if she did not already know what he was saying she would not have understood him now. She smiled sweetly at him before gesturing that she would follow her sister further up the tram, which she did leaving him to recover his seat in some confusion, sure that fellow passengers were all laughing at his clumsiness. Alice had not noticed what had happened and she remonstrated with her sister on hearing how the young man had become redder and redder until Caroline thought he would burst. Fortunately, when they came to leave the tram he had already gone, and they reached their destination without further incident.

The premises of the College for the Education and Promotion of Ladies in Medicine did not really mirror the grandeur of its title. It consisted of a grey end-terrace house rather the worse for wear, in a part of the town which had once been smart but had been in gradual decline for some years now. The additional disadvantage was that, to reach the house, students had to pass through an area of dilapidated tenements along a narrow street with broken cobbles rutted with cart tracks.

On the ground floor of the building part of the entrance hall had been fashioned to form a small office with a reception area. The remainder of the ground floor was mostly taken up by a large room used as an assembly room and also for some lectures. Upstairs were Miss Clegg's offices and some small rooms formerly bedrooms now to be used for individual study. The whole premises could have done with some redecoration but Alice and Caroline were too full of the excitement of the day to take note of that.

They were met in the reception area by a small rather round woman who introduced herself as Mrs Black, Miss Clegg's Secretary. In a rather peremptory way, she completed with them the necessary papers for their registration. Alice thought that Mrs Black appeared to give herself more importance than her position, not to mention her accent, seemed to justify. Alice quite prided herself on treating everyone equally but in fact she was not well pleased if they treated her as an equal in return. Caroline, for her part, reacted to Mrs Black's manner by dealing with her in an offhand way which was plainly not to the lady's liking. The initial registration was accordingly carried out with a coldness on both sides.

There were just under twenty other girls in the assembly room when they entered. Apart from one, the sisters knew them all more or less vaguely as living in the town. The one girl they did not know also rather stood out because she was a little older than the others. Her name was Margaret Campbell. She told the sisters she had come up from the country and that, although she had not previously known her, Miss Clegg had given her lodgings in her own house. Alice took to her straight away, possibly because they shared the same dark colouring and Margaret had a composed reflective way about her, always thinking before she spoke, which Alice found in tune with her own personality. As with all the girls Margaret had no medical background but, unlike the others, whose families were prosperous middle class and established, she was from a family of limited means, her parents running a small shop in the village where they lived.

Alice and Caroline sat beside one girl who introduced herself as Lucy Dalrymple. She was small and dark, with curly hair and a round face, made the more attractive by dimples when she smiled her frequent shy smile. Alice said to Caroline later that she was like a doll that you wanted to put up on the mantelshelf just to look at. Lucy had a bubbly personality which endeared her to those she met, and she and the sisters contributed to the general noise level which was rising when a door leading to an inner area opened and Miss Clegg strode in, with Mrs Black bobbing in her wake.

Miss Clegg had a spare figure which made her look taller than she was and her hair was drawn back from her face and tied behind in a bun. Her face was fixed in a stern mode and she was dressed in her usual black, emphasising the pallor of her skin. The chatter immediately died down as she made her way to stand by a desk in the bay window at the top of the room. Mrs Black sat down in a chair a little distance behind and to one side. Miss Clegg did not look at the girls assembled in front of her but stood with her eyes lowered as if she was composing herself. With every eye trained on her, fully a minute passed; and then another. Alice could hear a bird singing outside but inside not a sound. Finally, Miss Clegg spoke.

'Ladies, welcome to the College for the Education and Promotion of Ladies in Medicine. You have taken the first step on a road which I promise you is blocked by rocks and barriers that you will have to overcome. I know what you have to face because it is a road I myself have travelled and I bear the scars of that journey. We women, so often admired by men when we are in what they think of as our rightful sphere, soon lose their regard when we dare to stray into fields to which they think they have an exclusive right. Admiration is not just lost, it is replaced by dislike and ridicule. When their assumption of intellectual superiority is challenged, they react with derision; when it is overcome, they react with fury. As an example of this, in the course of my studies in New York, when I came out top in an examination of which I was the sole woman examinee, the authorities concealed the result for fear of exciting the anger of their male students.'

Miss Clegg's lips tightened at the memory, before she continued,

'Whether consciously or unconsciously men ascribe to us totally artificial standards of conduct and then express horror when we transgress them. Women, who, by virtue of bringing forth children, are privy to the most intimate details of the human body, are somehow shocking when that knowledge is to be publicly discussed.

'And yet men are totally inconsistent in their opposition. They are happy to let women of the lower classes toil and labour all day at back-breaking tasks and do not say that is not a female's place – that a woman is too weak for that. But we are expected to believe that somehow women of our class are too frail and slight to undertake work which requires a fraction of the strength which these other women have to use.

'A further consequence of this is that, to compensate for our assumed frailty, they proffer assistance where they would not do so to a man. When we come to a stile they will help us over it. This is the most poisoned of chalices. I cannot emphasise this enough. By accepting their assistance, we are confirming their prejudices. Everything we do, we must do using our own resources as women.'

Miss Clegg stopped there. A floorboard creaked as she moved to face out of the window as though deep in thought. Behind her, none of the girls dared to move. She turned to them again.

'Unfortunately, the opposition is not confined to men. Women, having been brought up to believe these absurd prejudices, are just as guilty when their beliefs are challenged. When I was studying in New York, the woman at whose house I was boarding, asked me to leave when she found out I was studying anatomy, as she said that I would give her establishment a bad name as a house of ill-repute.'

(Some of the girls smiled a little at that but speedily stopped when they realised Miss Clegg did not mean to be humorous.)

'The difficulties you will come up against are, accordingly, not physical ones but mental and spiritual ones and all the tougher because of that. You will suffer wounds and you will bear scars. You will have periods of dejection and periods when you don't want to go on. I know because that is what I have had to bear. Indeed, I still have to bear them because the battle is by no means won. It continues day by day and will continue until women achieve their proper place in the world.

'You may depend on it that you will be watched. Everything you do will be scrutinised to see if you make mistakes. And when you make mistakes they will be seized upon as evidence that you are not up to the task. We will never convince the doubters by argument, but your deeds will silence them.'

Again, she paused, looking over their heads to the back of the room as if in deep thought, while the girls kept their eyes transfixed on her.

'I am not a visionary. A visionary sees too far and then can lose heart as the journey seems to stretch on endlessly. I go up the hill, head down, one step at a time, secure in the knowledge that I can make that step; not sure when it will end. But I will know when I get to the top and I am given fresh strength knowing that you are now with me.

'A venture is dipping the toe in the water. An adventure is taking the full step and accepting the element of risk which is an essential part of it. You girls today are setting out on your adventure. You will require stout hearts and the keenest determination. I do not envy you the travails which lie ahead for you. But I do acclaim the courage you are showing in setting out. I wish you well'

With that Miss Clegg picked up her papers and stalked from the room leaving Mrs Black to speak to the girls.

Later that evening, as she was relating the events of the day to her parents and Anna, Caroline was almost bubbling over in her enthusiasm.

'Papa, you have no idea what she was like, 'She was like a general addressing his troops before a battle. I felt like cheering when she finished. She was like Henry V before Agincourt.'

Alice smiled at that, but she too had been much affected by Miss Clegg's words. She was diffident at expressing her reactions to her parents and indeed would have found difficulty in putting her thoughts into words. For some time, she had realised that, in some situations, words are inadequate to express feelings; they diminish what they describe. What she knew was that when Miss Clegg had referred to the spiritual challenge ahead, her whole being seemed to expand, and she realised more than ever that the choice she had made in pursuing medicine was the only one for her.

In talking further about Miss Clegg's speech, Alice told her parents of Miss Clegg's medical education in America. For reasons of decency she made no reference, in the presence of her father, to the house of ill-repute assertion, but her mother without saying anything pricked up her ears at her tale. Mrs Burton had never in her life met an American, but she had a low opinion of that country based entirely on the American episodes in Martin Chuzzlewit which she had read avidly when she was younger. Her suspicions of Miss Clegg were accordingly confirmed. 'You can't walk through a farmyard without getting mud on your skirt,' she said to herself. 'Just as I imagined.' But she said nothing and continued to listen to her daughters' accounts.

Caroline meantime was thinking impishly that if Miss Clegg was in a house of ill-repute it would not do much business, but she did not dare to share this thought even with her sister.

6

On that first assembly day, after Miss Clegg left, Mrs Black had taken over. She was socially inferior to most of the group and certainly their intellectual inferior and her awareness of this (because she was by no means stupid) made her attitude to them awkward, an awkwardness she tried but failed to conceal, by aping Miss Clegg's normal stern manner. She handed out details of the classes they were to attend and the courses they were to follow and there was a general hubbub which she tried to quell as the girls read through the papers and took in what was involved. She called for their attention and then tried to set down rules as to how they were to behave. This did not go down well with some of the girls who felt they were well aware of how to comport themselves. But Mrs Black ignored the reaction and pressed on to stress the necessity of punctuality and regularity of attendance at their classes.

She emphasised, in particular, that they would throughout their studies come into contact with male students following similar courses and that on no account were they to approach them. Caroline interjected to say that she didn't know about Mrs Black's experience, but she had always found that it to be the men who did the approaching. The other girls giggled, but Mrs Black was not pleased and reported later to Miss Clegg that there was a troublemaker in the class.

When Mrs Black returned to her little office she carefully put away the papers relating to each girl, each in its previously prepared place. She was still trembling with indignation at the way some of the students had failed to give her the respect she regarded as her entitlement and had treated her almost as a servant. 'We'll soon sort that out' she said to herself. 'They'll either dance to ma tune or they willnae dance at a'. A'll mak' quite sure o' that.'

Miss Clegg was meantime sitting in her study, her back, ramrod straight, not touching the back of her chair. Her desk was clear of papers and any of the usual bric-a-brac normally expected on an office desk. In this it reflected the clarity of her mind which she had schooled to keep different matters totally separate so that when dealing with something she could bend all her concentration on that topic without distraction. The only exception on the desk was a small polished box, something she had a habit of stroking almost as an aid to thought when she was thinking deeply.

At this moment, almost at the culmination of all her efforts, she had expected to feel euphoric but instead she felt empty, almost uneasy. She had been brought up in a home where a much loved, talented mother had been systematically ground down by years of abuse from a husband whose only claim to superiority over her was in being a man and therefore could control her every action, and who bolstered his inadequacy by turning to alcohol for support. Amongst his friends, he was regarded as quite a fellow, always up for a jape, but what went on within the home was kept hidden from the world. And what Jennifer Clegg felt, as she grew up, was also hidden from the world. In consequence, she was used to being alone and indeed thought of this as a strength. But after her speech she felt lonely as she sat on her chair. If only Mary Jane were here, she thought - and then almost physically dashed the thought from her mind by rising to her feet and moving to the window.

She turned her mind back to the day's events. When warning the girls of the difficulties they would face she had also hinted at how she herself was still beset with problems. One of these had arisen at a very late stage when that silly Lucy Dalrymple had failed two papers in the preliminary examination, the passing of which the General Medical Council had made a necessary part of embarking on a course of medical study. This meant had left Miss Clegg short of the minimum number of students which the Trustees of the College had laid down to make the College viable and therefore the College would not be able to operate. Miss Clegg did not waste her time arguing with the Trustees, whom she regarded in any event as a disagreeable necessity, but in the short time available to her, she carried out considerable research into the regulations. In this, without her knowledge, she was aided by Dr Ring who was going to lecture to the girls on Materia Medica, and who also happened to be the Secretary of the College of Physicians. Miss Clegg regarded him as a spineless individual, but it was he who was able to establish that, provided Lucy passed the subjects at a subsequent date, she would be able to start her medical course. When this confirmation reached Miss Clegg, she was able to inform the Trustees that the College could open.

Miss Clegg did not know it was through Dr Ring's efforts that a concession had been made allowing Lucy to start her course without the required certificate. Had she known that it was a concession obtained solely because it was for a female student she would have rejected the move, whether or not the whole project would then have foundered.

And then that very morning, just before she went to address the girls, she had received a note from Baillie Macnair whom she had persuaded to join the Board of Trustees. She did not particularly like him, but she felt that his presence on the Board gave it some much needed standing. Now, on the very day of the opening, he had written to say that because of pressure of work he would have to resign his position. Miss Clegg knew it was nothing to do with pressure of work. He had joined because, as an uneducated man, he felt that being a Trustee boosted his standing in the community. He now resigned because he felt that the adverse publicity which the enterprise was gaining was actually having the reverse effect.

Miss Clegg felt contempt for his weakness, but she would soldier on. Her first task was to imbue the girls with some of her own spirit. She had heard with some distaste the hubbub of chatter in the Assembly Room before she entered, and which was renewed after she left. They were like wild horses needing to be tamed to serve any useful purpose. The girls were willing, but they had not been tempered by adversity as she had. The discipline which had been grafted into her very being, would have to be imposed on them externally through her leadership. That rather than any medical training was going to be Miss Clegg's main focus.

7

The day after the first assembly was the first real day of study. Accompanied to the tram stop by Anna as their 'guardian' the girls again travelled by tram, which Alice assured her father was so much better because it ran on rails, giving a much smoother ride than a carriage on the normal cobbles. He let that pass but Mrs Burton was still horrified. She was not sure what was worse, her daughters studying medicine or being seen using public transport. In addition, the tram route, although starting in the leafy surroundings where the Burtons lived, then made its way between high tenement buildings. These, at one time, had been occupied by the well-to-do but, as the wealthy gradually moved out to the new suburbs, were now home to the poorer classes crammed much more thickly into what had once been elegant dwellings. The streets, too, became increasingly noisy and dirty, more and more crowded with people, many of a type that Mrs Burton did not feel her daughters should be near, unescorted, even from the safe distance of the tram. And some of these people, merely by paying the fare, could board the tram and, without seeking permission, take a seat right beside her daughters. She felt it completely intolerable.

On their way to the College, after leaving the tram, the sisters met an acquaintance who was intrigued by what they were doing, and they spent a few moments with her discussing their plans. As a result, they were a few minutes late in arriving at the College although well in time for the lecture. They were greeted at the Reception by Mrs Black who remonstrated with them at their lateness. Alice pointed out that they were in good time for the lecture, but Mrs Black insisted, over their protestations, that, although the lecture did not start until 9.30, Miss Clegg had laid down that all students were required to register with Reception before 9 o' clock every morning. From differing points of view, both Mrs Black and the girls regarded this as a bad start and it was with strained politeness that the sisters passed on into the Assembly Room.

Although the female students were to pursue roughly the same course as the male students, it had been decided by the authorities that it would be indelicate for the male and female students to attend lectures together. Miss Clegg had indicated to her students that in her view it was not fear of indecency but fear of competition which lay behind the decision, but it had to be accepted. Some of the lectures were held in the same university rooms as those attended by the male students most often running one after the other. Only the anatomy class, which was to be given by Miss Clegg, and the class on Materia Medica, which was to be their first lecture, were to be held in the College premises.

'Materia Medica is the study of the source, constituents, and chemical and physical characteristics of the organic and inorganic materials used for drugs in the practice of medicine.'

Thus, Dr Ring began his first lecture to the assembled class. He was a man of medium height, with wispy fair hair and a slightly apologetic manner. One of those people who seem to go through life cringing from an expected attack, they almost invite it and because of that they suffer more than most. He never said he had been bullied at school, but he must have been. After the premature death of both his parents he had been brought up by maiden aunts who, early on, decided that their main duty was to inculcate in him a total knowledge of Holy Scripture. In this they were successful, but at the same time his natural abilities meant he was able to shine in other less restricted disciplines, enabling him in due course to obtain his university degree.

Materia Medica deals with the nature and actions of drugs and rational treatment of disease with further extension into toxicology, in which drugs move into the realm of poison. It can also delve into the field of homeopathic medicine and even into faith healing taking into account the old maxim that nature heals, physicians treat. It can be a fascinating subject of study in the hands of a skilled lecturer. Dr Ring was not such a lecturer. Although he was pre-eminent in his field he was renowned as the worst lecturer in the medical faculty. His parents, showing a lack of foresight they had possibly passed on to him, had had him christened Brian Oliver and it was inevitable that he became known in due course as Dr Boring, by staff and students alike.

In his lectures to male students he was accustomed to restive audiences who indulged in boisterous sometimes downright rude behaviour with which he was totally unable to cope. Miss Clegg had little time for him, but he was prepared to take on work in her College thinking that, although he rather quailed before her, he would get a more receptive hearing from the young ladies. This was not to prove the case. It was not long, even in this first lecture, before he began to pick up the familiar signs of inattention, with much shuffling of feet and gazing out of the window. It made for a long lecture only enlivened for Caroline by his pronunciation of the words 'accuracy' and 'accurate' which he pronounced 'ackeracy' and 'ackerate'. She began to look forward to their use and, as accuracy is an important element in the preparation of drugs, the words occurred satisfactorily frequently and could be seen coming to the delight of Caroline and her immediate neighbours.

At the end of the lecture there was an audible sigh of relief from the students which was at least better for Dr Ring than the hurrahs he was accustomed to get from the male students. The female students were mostly subdued not to say depressed, as they filed past him on the way out, their eyes cast down. Only Lucy acknowledged him. With her generous nature, she had quickly realised he was uncomfortable in giving his lecture and she went out of her way to thank him as she was leaving. In turn, Dr Ring recognised Lucy as the student whom he had helped to gain entry to the course, but he was so put off by this unaccustomed approach that he managed to drop on the floor most of the papers which he had been gathering. With a smile, she helped him to pick them up.

Outside the lecture room Caroline and Alice were waiting for her and queried why it had taken her so long. When Lucy explained that she had been thanking Dr Ring, Alice raised her eyebrows in disbelief while Caroline said that the only thanking due was to thank God that it was all over.

8

The girls now made their way to their next lecture, which was on anatomy, the class to be given by Miss Clegg. The contrast could not have been more dramatic. Admittedly anatomy as a subject perhaps holds more immediate attraction than Materia Medica but in addition Miss Clegg, for all her faults, was a born teacher. In this first lecture, she merely gave an introduction to the whole subject putting it in context with other parts of their course and getting the students to think of their bodies in a new way. Then towards the end of the lecture she moved towards what appeared to be a statue covered with a rug before dramatically tearing off the covering to reveal a human skeleton. The gasps from the girls were sufficient sign that her trick had been successful, and she was able to bring home to them that, male and female, this was the structure on which their whole learning had to be based. Miss Clegg then left, leaving them with the skeleton.

The girls were slow to disperse, taking time to approach the skeleton with some like Lucy being much more diffident in drawing near. As they left, Lucy was horrified when Caroline teasingly said to her from now on that every time she looked at her now all she would see was her bones.

The next lecture was on chemistry and would take place in the university precincts which, like the College, were in the old part of the town, as the university had been established many centuries ago, with the town growing round it. On their way there, they encountered some male students who were coming from their own chemistry lecture and the girls were taken aback by the reaction of some of the men to them. There were loud comments some verging on the obscene, and the girls' way was from time to time obstructed, forcing them to go onto the road. Alice recognised one of the worst offenders a man called John Common, who was the son of a doctor and whom Alice had known since they were children.

'Did you see him, Caroline? Do you remember him as a child when he used to bully the other children? He hasn't changed a bit.'

This was the first time the girls had experienced the animosity Miss Clegg had warned them to expect and they clung together for support. Lucy was the most affected. She was visibly trembling and needed the comforting arms of Alice and Margaret Campbell to console her. However, not all of the men had behaved badly and indeed most smiled and nodded to the girls as they met them.

Suddenly Lucy, who had quickly recovered her good spirits, cried out, 'There's Roddy'

Alice and Caroline didn't know what she meant but she approached one of the men and brought him over to be introduced to the sisters as a sort of cousin of hers. Alice thought he looked vaguely familiar, but Caroline realised right away that he was the man who had tried to offer her a seat on the tram. If she had not immediately recognised him she would have quickly done so now, as he turned the same deep red colour and mumbled just as indistinctly as he had done before. Neither mentioned the previous encounter. Although he listened to her conversation with Lucy, he avoided her gaze, and, after exchanging a few words with Lucy tipped his hat to them and made good his escape.

Lucy explained that he was related to her through her father's side of the family. He lived in the country, but she had not really known him until comparatively recently, during her late father's final illness, when he had visited her father a lot and had, she said, brought enormous comfort to her mother. As she was telling this Lucy's eyes welled up but Caroline soon got her over it, by teasing that he might be called Roddy but she would call him Ruddy because that was the way he was whenever she saw him. And, although Lucy had explained that his father was the village headmaster, Caroline insisted, to the girls' amusement, that he must be, in fact, the local shepherd and the reason he was tongue-tied was that he was more used to talking to his sheep.

By this time the remaining men had gone on their way and, chattering light-heartedly, the girls made their way to their next lecture.

9

Roderick John MacDonald, or Roddy John as he was known in the Highland village in which he lived, was indeed the son of the local schoolmaster whose wife had died giving birth to Roddy who was her only child, and he had been brought up by his father and his father's unmarried sister. For this reason, and because he spent more time reading than most of his friends, he had always felt a little apart from them even when he was playing the same games as. His decision to go to university to study medicine set him even further apart. Despite this, his friends took a keen interest in his progress and took pride in the reports they got from his father about his activities in the big city.

A further consequence of his detachment from the full village life was that he was socially inexperienced and a little awkward, especially where girls were concerned. Someone as tall as Roddy is somehow expected to be master of every situation but, while that might come in time, he still had some learning to do.

When he first came to the city he gradually got to know some of his fellow students and because of his size he was welcomed early on by the rugby enthusiasts, a sport just starting to gain a footing at the university. He loved the rough and tumble of the game and also took a full part in the drinking bouts which generally followed. Indeed, Roddy developed a reputation as a formidable drinker especially as he was rumoured to be able to return to his lodgings after a hard session and delve straight into his studies, at which he excelled.

He did not, however, enjoy the coarse behaviour which many of his fellow students indulged in. For example, he was offended when one of his group, John Common, referred to someone they had just met as a 'Jew Boy', but, still at the stage of trying to be thought of as part of the group and (although he was ashamed of it), he said nothing. The psychology of a group very often involves shared beliefs and to dispute these entails banishment from the group. As a stranger in the city Roddy welcomed the companionship of the group and at first tolerated their views as a price to be paid for being part of it.

One of their most rigidly held beliefs was that women had no place in medicine and that any woman who wished to study medicine had no moral standards and had forfeited her right to be treated as a lady. Before he came up to university Roddy had not even known that there were women who wished to study at university, far less wishing to become doctors. When he thought about it now, and not all that carefully, he could see no good reason why they shouldn't do as they wished. Of one thing he was certain: whatever they chose to do they were entitled to the same courtesy as other women – and, indeed other men.

For this reason, although he kept up the rugby and as he made friends with more congenial company, he gradually moved away from the original group. They were aware of his distancing and of his unstated disapproval and resented it accordingly.

When Roddy had risen to offer Caroline his seat in the tram, he was merely doing something which came naturally to him; he would have done the same for any woman young or old. But even as he was mumbling and shuffling he was sufficiently conscious to be aware that she was very attractive, with a lissom figure which he followed with his eyes as she moved further up the tram. Now, when he met her again, he still bumbled and flushed even as he took in just how pretty she was. His problem was that, just as he had decided on something to contribute to the general conversation, Caroline had flitted to another topic, leaving his laboriously worked out bon mot stuck in his mouth. He would later run over this first proper meeting in his mind with his comments nicely in place, but that was not how it was at the time.

The archetypal lover is dark and slim with an elegant charm; prone to melancholy and losing interest in food when spurned by his mistress. Roddy had none of these characteristics and indeed, if anything, his appetite increased. But he was without doubt a lover even though he did not think of himself in that sense. He could not, even if he would, have described her nose or her mouth or her eyes. He just knew that when he saw Caroline he felt enveloped in a glow of happiness and warmth. Just to see her, even in the distance, made for him a perfect day.

He learned from Lucy roughly what her weekly programme was and made every effort to be in the area when she was coming to classes. Caroline had a particularly graceful walk with a vigorous stride slightly longer than is normal in a woman and he loved to watch her as she moved along. Caroline was not aware of the way that she walked but she was aware that Lucy's friend Roddy was regularly to be seen although, unless Lucy was with her, they didn't exchange any words.

Roddy congratulated himself that Caroline would not be conscious of his interest. In truth, he would have been embarrassed if she had. But Alice, being her sister, recognised that it was not by chance that they kept on meeting Roddy, and joked with her that she had a swain, an idea which Caroline rather liked. Although she still kept on referring to him as Ruddy, she started to quite enjoy his distant attention and was content to leave it at that, until Lucy mentioned that Roddy had been to visit her at her family home and how pleasant she thought he was. This put a different complexion on things. Caroline may have regarded him, in Alice's words, as a puppy, but he was her puppy, nobody else's, and she quietly determined to pull in his lead somewhat.

Whenever the weather allowed it, the sisters left the tram a few stops earlier to walk part of the way to the College through the park known as James Fields. Now, whenever she knew that Roddy was coming behind them, Caroline would stop to bring Alice's attention to some bush or other which ensured that Roddy had then to overtake them. At first this manoeuvre merely resulted in Roddy tipping his hat as he passed them but gradually a few words would be exchanged until eventually it became natural for him to join them in walking towards the University buildings. Through time he stopped turning red whenever he met them and through time Caroline stopped referring to him as Ruddy, although she still persisted in her myth that he was the local shepherd.

10

Life at the College settled down to a routine of lectures and study. In their day-to-day activities, Alice and Caroline chiefly came into contact with Mrs Black as they had to register with her when they arrived in the morning. Mrs Black disapproved of their timekeeping, their mode of dress, their light-heartedness. Indeed, she disapproved of them generally, possibly because their behaviour differed so much from that of Miss Clegg whom Mrs Black regarded as little short of a god (or possibly a goddess) and as the pattern to which all medical ladies should conform. Just to annoy them she pointedly looked at the clock whenever they arrived, and she affected not to remember their names whenever they presented themselves in the morning.

Although Mrs Black irritated even her, Alice tried to explain to Caroline that her assistance's devotion to Miss Clegg showed a loyal heart, and this was a point in her favour. 'If you take all a person's bad points' she told her sister 'and put them together, you will have a bad person and you are entitled to dislike her. But that is a distortion of that person. We all have good points and bad points, and to be fair you have to take them all into consideration.'

Caroline was not to be persuaded. Mrs Black's first name was Roberta and, as she always dressed in black, Caroline had taken to calling her Black Bob and it was as Black Bob that she became known to the whole class. 'Where Black Bob is concerned, I don't see the need to be fair, as you call it. I like to dislike her.'

Caroline was unfair to Mrs Black who wore black simply because she was a widow. Caroline, like all of the class, was too young and inexperienced to appreciate the difficult position that Mrs Black was in. She had formerly worked in Miss Clegg's house and was overjoyed when, on the opening of the College, Miss Clegg appointed her as her Secretary. It was a position she prized and which she never failed to mention when she was in the company of her friends, but it gave her a stature she had difficulty in sustaining in the College. She could read and write but had never lost the habit of following the words she was reading with her finger and mouthing them with her lips. She was also prone to malapropisms and the occasional mixed metaphor, on one occasion combining three when she told the students - to their delight - that the future of the College was hanging in the melting point.

The students, like all young people, were merciless in probing the weaknesses of those placed in authority, and amongst themselves made fun of her mannerisms and her accent which, under stress, slipped from her carefully acquired diction back to her native Doric. They also, it is shameful to say, played tricks on her; on one occasion introducing a field mouse into the drawer of her desk and waiting for her scream when she opened it. No-one owned up to that prank, but Alice had her suspicions.

Mrs Black's only defence was to carry out her duties punctiliously. She looked after Miss Clegg's correspondence efficiently and kept what she referred to as 'ma registrar' scrupulously, recording the exact number of minutes a student was over time and berating them for their lateness. She had authority but no power. All she could do was to report back to Miss Clegg - sometimes with embellishments, because she was only human - on the misdeeds of the students. Because of this she was generally regarded by the students as a spy.

One person who was seen regularly at the College was Dr Boring, as he gave his Materia Medica lectures there. The girls were scarcely aware of him as he still passed them with his nearly soundless walk and with his head lowered so as to avoid face to face contact. The only exception was Lucy who, after initially speaking to him at the first lecture, had gone out of her way to befriend him. She developed the habit of going into his lecture room early to assist him in setting up his materials and staying on afterwards to help him in clearing up. When she was doing this, she would talk away quite naturally about her home life and about what she hoped to achieve.

She told him about her beloved father and how it was the long drawn out illness leading to his death that had spurred her into applying to study medicine, an application which he had encouraged. Dr Ring, who had never married, was very moved when she talked of her love for her father and how she was devastated by his death which had taken place right in the middle of the examinations the previous year.

He felt that in some small way he was taking the place of her father and this conceit filled him with enormous pleasure so that he actually looked forward to his lectures, something which had never happened before. And his giving of the lectures in fact improved, although his students perhaps did not notice the difference.

While Miss Clegg's presence pervaded the whole College, they saw little of her apart from her lectures in anatomy. Most of her time she spent in her study dealing with the enormous amount of correspondence in which she was engaged chiefly with those who, like her, were involved in the struggle to improve the position of women in every sphere. The students were only physically conscious of her if she came out of her study, usually to reprimand, with a look, someone who was not showing what Miss Clegg regarded as the proper attitude to her studies. But there was no doubt that she was the framework upon which the whole structure was built.

Her lectures continued to enthral the students. They brought home to Alice, in particular, that, when she first expressed the desire to become a doctor, all she had in mind was a general vague idea of bringing solace to people. But now she had the feeling that, with her new knowledge, she could have a practical effect on the sick, not just bring them comfort.

She also realised that what she was learning was having a significant effect on how she saw herself and other people, no more so than when Miss Clegg introduced them to the male body and reproduction. She had previously lectured on the female body and its organs but that was something about which the students obviously had practical if somewhat vague knowledge. The male body, to all but those who had younger brothers, was a total mystery. When Miss Clegg showed them woodcuts of the male genitalia, Alice fully understood why the male and female students were separated in the anatomy class. It was bad enough looking at these drawings in the company of other girls.

There was always attention in the anatomy class because the students were engrossed in what they were learning but when Miss Clegg went on to describe the process by which the penis became stiff and penetrated the vagina before ejaculating the semen the silence was profound with the girls concentrating on their books and avoiding eye contact with their classmates. And when Miss Clegg finished and left the room there was none of the usual hubbub as students checked to see whether they had missed anything and discussed what they had learned. Rather, they left the room individually and went on their way without speaking. Even Caroline, who normally could be relied upon to raise a giggle about some aspect of a past lecture, said nothing; and it was some time before the students, as a whole, became comfortable with their new knowledge. Alice and Caroline did later discuss things with Anna although one topic was never raised, even though it was in their minds - the realisation that their parents must have done all this, for them to be born.

Eventually, though, even Lucy had the confidence to make an allusion to '*that* lecture' as she called it. She said that for some time after it she could not look a man in the face. Caroline's response was that, for her, it was the only part of his body she *could* look at. Alice was not amused.

11

Although the students as a body reverenced Miss Clegg, they did not know her and felt her remoteness, a remoteness she encouraged. The only girl who knew a little more about Miss Clegg was the student who lodged with her and whom Alice had taken an immediate liking to when she had met her on the first day, Margaret Campbell

Margaret was inspired, in her early education, by two maiden sisters, the Misses Dunlop, who had retired in their older years to their native village. Learning that they had worked with Florence Nightingale in the Crimea Margaret Campbell had first determined to become a nurse following their lead. And then she learnt through the older, Miss Dunlop, who carried on a copious correspondence with many of her former colleagues, that there were one or two pioneering women who had taken the final step of becoming medically qualified. There was a dream! And it would have remained a dream had not Miss Dunlop and Miss Jean shared the dream. More and more letters went out and were received, communications were made, contacts were used.

One of those who became involved in the correspondence was Miss Clegg and eventually it was agreed that Margaret could board with her free of charge in return for her carrying out some secretarial duties in the house, with the two old sisters meeting the cost of the tuition fees. This latter arrangement, Margaret, with her independent spirit, refused at first but her old friends persuaded her that she could not deny them the pleasure of seeing, achieved through her, what they could never have hoped for themselves.

All the arrangements for Margaret had been done through her old friends so that the first time she met Miss Clegg was when she arrived at her door to start her stay.

When she presented herself, she was told to wait in the parlour while Miss Clegg was fetched. The parlour was, like the house itself, very neat, being sparsely furnished with none of the loose ornaments which at that time frequently cluttered up public rooms in houses. Miss Clegg's welcome was equally spare.

'You must be Miss Campbell. I hope you had a pleasant journey. The maid will show you to your room. We have breakfast here at 7 o'clock sharp and our evening meal at quarter to seven. I will discuss with you later what your duties will be.'

Each of the above sentences would normally be followed by a gap allowing the other party an opportunity at least to nod if not to speak in acknowledgement but Miss Clegg obviously did not consider this necessary and she left the room leaving Margaret alone and slightly nonplussed. All her own words of greeting and messages to Miss Clegg from her old village friends were left unsaid, and Margaret just had to follow the maid to her room. She was so taken aback that, while she would normally have exchanged a few words with the maid on the way there, she remained silent until the maid left her.

She felt a little dejected as she sat on her bed, and a little discouraged. She had naturally been apprehensive in setting out on this adventure, which was the first time she had journeyed away from her village on her own and had maybe expected a warmer welcome to reassure her. Then after a bit she muttered, 'Give yourself a shake. If you had been coming to stay as a lodger with a normal landlady this is what you might have expected.'

And she sat down to write to her old friends to confirm her arrival - although she gave a slightly more positive slant on Miss Clegg's welcome.

After this start Margaret quickly learned that the house was run on rigid lines. Breakfast was indeed at 7 o'clock sharp but Margaret was aware that Miss Clegg herself was up and about by 5 o'clock every morning and, as she rarely was in bed until midnight at the earliest, she seemed to be able to survive on very little sleep. On College days Miss Clegg left at 8.30 and returned at 5.30. She then worked in her study until dinner time and after dinner returned to her study. At 9.30 the staff and Margaret were assembled for evening prayers led by Miss Clegg, consisting of a reading from Scripture, which in course of time Margaret was permitted to give, an extract from an improving book chosen by Miss Clegg, and, after some five minutes of private prayer, a final plea for a blessing. Thereafter Miss Clegg again retired to her study and the rest of the household went to bed.

Everything in the house had its proper place. Early on, Margaret made the mistake of taking out one of the many books on the bookshelves and, as she had not finished it, marking her position in it with a card and leaving it out. She was reprimanded that books should always be returned to their correct position and on no account, should they have page markers in them.

Miss Clegg was severe on the staff although to be fair she was merely expecting them to abide by standards by which she herself lived. But the servants were just human and, while Margaret was in residence, there was a regular turnover, including those in the kitchen where there was none to be found to meet Miss Clegg's exacting standards.

This turnover of staff applied also at the College where the students became used to seeing a new man working at the fires just weeks after his predecessor had started. The only exception to this was Mrs Black, who apparently had been with Miss Clegg for years. Caroline suggested it was a devil's pact, and it was certainly striking, though, of course, there was no possibility of raising the matter with Mrs Black.

At the house, Miss Clegg continued to call Margaret 'Miss Campbell' (and indeed did so throughout her entire stay) but gradually her attitude became less impersonal. She approved of Margaret's studious nature and was also intrigued by her skill in sewing and needlework. At first Margaret had the impression (probably correctly) that Miss Clegg did not approve of her sewing, on the basis that it was a feminine pursuit and therefore could be interpreted as too frivolous, but, as Miss Clegg saw the high degree of skill and artistry involved, she took a real interest, especially when Margaret explained that the work she was engaged on was for young relatives of her old village friends.

If Margaret had come to stay with free lodgings on the basis that she would do some work for Miss Clegg, it became clear that Miss Clegg saw no real need for any help and had made the offer merely as a favour. This did not sit well with Margaret. As she gained Miss Clegg's confidence she eventually was given access to the holy of holies,

Miss Clegg's study, and once there realised that the neatness and tidiness of the rest of the house (and indeed of Miss Clegg's room at the College) did not extend here. Despite Miss Clegg's protests Margaret made it her job to bring some order into the chaos and, because they shared the same disciplined nature, this satisfied both parties.

Most people regarded Miss Clegg's attitude as offensive and aggressive but, through living with her, Margaret came to realise that it was really her defensive armour against anticipated attacks from opponents. In the house, now that she was more relaxed with Margaret, she would occasionally admit to weariness. In particular, from time to time, after a major crisis, Miss Clegg suffered from excruciating headaches leaving her almost unable to speak, and with jagged lines interfering with her vision. She had not dared tell anyone, especially the servants, in case it became public and be used against her, but, as she knew her better and trusted her, she confessed to Margaret. When this first happened, Margaret felt unable to do anything apart from giving sympathy as she knew that Miss Clegg hated to be touched. Subsequently Margaret was permitted to lead her into her bedroom and assist her by keeping the room dark, easing her clothing, putting a cold compress on her forehead and making sure that everything was kept totally quiet.

The life which Margaret led in the house was quiet and would not have suited many girls of her age but Margaret, being reflective by nature and used to being left to her own devices, was content. When she did go out and about, she occasionally met some of the neighbours who were always curious about their famous, or infamous, neighbour, a curiosity which Margaret made no attempt to satisfy. Mrs MacNeil who lived next door was particularly curious and persistent and one day, in the way of the practised gossip, she proffered a titbit to encourage confidences in return.

'It was a shame about the previous young lady who lived with Miss Clegg. Nice young lady although not very strong. She was called Mary Jane. I don't know what her surname was.' As this provoked no reaction from Margaret, she went on, 'She just seemed to fade away.'

Margaret could not help but ask, 'You mean she left?'

'Oh no, she died. Such a shame.'

Margaret assured Mrs MacNeil that she was extremely strong and had no intention of dying, then she turned the conversation to something more general, somewhat to Mrs MacNeil's frustration.

Margaret, although intrigued by the story, had no intention of raising the matter with Miss Clegg and thought she would ask, when she was next in College, if the other girls they knew anything about it.

12

Although some of the girls were inquisitive about what Miss Clegg was like at home, Margaret never responded to their probing, even when Caroline went on one of her flights of fancy. In the morning after Margaret's chat with Mrs MacNeil, Caroline continued her exposition on Miss Clegg's clothing, explaining she no longer thought that Miss Clegg had only one black dress - Caroline now thought she had a few and was sewn into one on a Monday morning and had it removed only on Friday evening.

Whilst Margaret assured the girls that Caroline's speculation was totally false, she did take the opportunity to ask if anyone knew anything about Miss Clegg's former lodger, Mary Jane. She did so a little warily, knowing she might spark off another leap in Caroline's imagination. However, no one seemed to know anything or be much interested. They were too much taken up in the excitement of the preparations for the next day.

This was to be their first examination in anatomy and was take place in the Apothecaries Hall a little distance from the College. It had an additional dimension for the girls as the male students were sitting the same exam at the same time although at a separate venue. This was a chance to show what they could do in competition.

Most of the girls normally walked to the College from their homes, and all but one of them had to pass the Apothecaries Hall on their way to the College. Thus, they resented having to go first to the College to register, before re tracing their steps to the Hall. The connecting roads were heavily congested, with horse-drawn vehicles of varying sizes, and hand-pulled carts to add to the confusion. In the mornings, they were crowded and still often strewn with overnight rubbish. Eventually Alice was deputed to approach Miss Clegg to see whether the students could go direct to the exam. As support, Alice agreed that Caroline could accompany her - on the strict understanding that she should say nothing.

One irritating aspect of how the College was run was that any approach to Miss Clegg had to be made through Mrs Black. When the girls explained their business to

Mrs Black she said there could be no departure from the normal rule and she saw no need for them to speak to Miss Clegg. She regarded their insistence on speaking direct to Miss Clegg as yet another example of their refusal to accept her authority. And so it was, but the sisters, and indeed the class as a whole, resented Mrs Black's assertion of authority in any event.

Mrs Black went into Miss Clegg's study before ushering them in and Alice could easily surmise that she did not do so with the intention of smoothing their path.

Miss Clegg was behind her desk, as usual sitting bolt upright on her chair, Mrs Black standing behind her arms crossed and her lips compressed. Miss Clegg did not ask the girls to sit. Nor did she say anything. Alice was waiting for her to speak and when she didn't there was an awkward silence before Alice herself had to start.

'It's about the arrangements for the examination tomorrow.'

'I am aware of the examination and Mrs Black tells me that all arrangements are properly in place.'

'The girls were wondering whether, instead of coming to the College first, they could go direct to Apothecaries Hall. Nearly all of us pass the Hall on our way here. Lucy Dalrymple, in fact, lives within fifty yards of the Hall. It seems a bit silly to have to come here first.' As soon as she used the word 'silly' Alice could have bitten her tongue off, but it was too late.

'I'm sorry that you find the arrangements I make to be silly. It may be that there are other establishments where you might find arrangements more suitable to you. The ones I have made for my establishment here remain in place'

Alice tried to say something in reply but to no avail and for once Caroline, who so wanted to come to her sister's rescue, had the sense to keep quiet.

'Thank you, Mrs Black for bringing this matter to my attention. Good day to you.' And with that Miss Clegg turned her attention to some papers on her desk leaving the sisters to make their retreat, thoroughly crestfallen.

The other girls crowded around them when they returned but, with Mrs Black hovering in the background, they merely reported that the request had been turned down. Once she had left, Alice told of the coldness of their reception. She had gone to see Miss Clegg with, possibly, a sense of her own importance as a spokeswoman for the class and she was completely deflated by the way she had been dismissed. As she told the other girls, 'She really treated us like disobedient children who had to be disciplined.'

Alice could not say more as she was so upset. Caroline was furious that her much loved sister whom Caroline, for all her jokes, looked up to, had been humiliated in this way.

All her efforts to revive Alice's spirits took some time to have effect and it was late on in the day before Alice fully recovered her composure.

On the morning of the exam, the girls gathered as they had been told, at the College. There was much nervous excitement, with exchanges of concern as to how they would fare. There was also talk about how they were not the only people aware of the exam. The local popular newspaper the Daily Register (or Daily Rag as Caroline called it) had been carrying out a campaign against the training of lady medical practitioners calling it an affront to morals and an indication of how the ethical standards of the nation had slipped since the glorious days of its forefathers. It highlighted this exam as another milepost on the path to perdition. Although they would not have admitted at home to reading such a newspaper, most of the girls had access to a copy some way or another and they were aware of the campaign, which they treated with a mixture of indignation and scorn. They knew, accordingly, that what in theory was a private exam had been turned, by the reports, into a public event.

As the girls started to leave the College Alice gestured to her sister to hold back a little.

'You know all this rubbish in the newspaper about medical women. Well I think it is going to make us look conspicuous if the whole group of us, all roughly the same age, all quite well dressed, go up the street in a convoy. We will merely draw attention to ourselves. Let's just wait a bit.'

Accordingly, the sisters left several moments after the others. After a few hundred yards Alice said to Caroline, 'The streets are very busy this morning. There must be something on.'

A little later Caroline replied, 'I think we must be the something which is on. People are definitely watching us. And I've noticed that some have started to follow us.'

They couldn't understand what was happening but the whole effect was to make the girls uneasy and they decided to stick closely together especially as there was no sign of the other girls who had left before them. Soon they were forming part of a growing crowd as they went along and out of the crowd they heard a voice cry,

'There's more of them. There they are!'

And from all sides now there came shouts and jeers.

The girls unconsciously quickened their step to get to Apothecary Lane a narrow lane leading to the Hall. When they turned into it they found the press of people was such that they had difficulty in making progress. The shouting became louder and more distinct.

'Strumpets,' came from one voice. 'All that finery and they're only after one thing.'

'Go back to where you belong...'

'That one in front - it's her only chance of getting her hands on a man...'

'It's her only chance of getting her hands on a cock...'

'She can have mine if she wants...'

This last produced hoarse laughter but the cries of 'scum' and 'whores' continued.

'Sticks and stones' whispered Alice to Caroline, and, holding hands, they pressed on. Although there was still no sign of the other girls, the gates of the Hall, and with them sanctuary, were just ahead. A few steps more and they were there.

But the gates were locked.

The sisters turned in despair, by now really frightened, but the mob jostled and jammed them against the railings. They turned back to the gates and saw John

Common through the gates - and he had the key. They were safe. But to their horror, he made no move to help them. Despite their desperate pleas for assistance he merely brandished the key at them; he and his cronies laughing and joking at their predicament.

The noise was increasing. Despite the early hour, many of the crowd, both male and female, had been drinking and they pushed and shoved to get a better view. Some picked up bits of rubbish to throw. Alice and Caroline were actually swept away from the gates by the swaying of the crowd. A mob has a life of its own. It often starts off in good humour with people quite enjoying jostling for position, then as feet are stood on and shoving becomes tougher it becomes bad-tempered. After that, it becomes independent of the people and sways and surges like the sea, carrying people along as in a rip tide. Alice and Caroline had great difficulty in keeping their feet. There was one mighty surge and the girls' grip on each other's hands was broken.

Alice quickly lost sight of Caroline in the tumult. The air was heavy with sweat, and the dust which was being kicked up; Caroline could feel it in her throat. Turning to see whether she could catch sight of Alice, she lost a shoe. She could feel the pressure of the weight of the crowd on her chest and tried to turn so as to take the force sideways on. A second later the angle of the pressure altered, and she again felt her chest compressed so that she could hardly breathe. The bodice of her dress was torn. The noise in her ears was deafening. Eventually, the press of the crowd lifted her off her feet. With her last remaining strength, Caroline tried to beat off hands which were grabbing at her and her clothing.

Then blackness.

13

The next thing Caroline knew was grass against her cheek. She slowly became conscious of the sun shining in her eyes and that she was lying in the open air on a grassy mound. As she turned her head painfully she saw Alice kneeling beside her. Then the memory of the noise and the smell and the crowd returned. She tried to get up only to be held down by Alice.

'Where am I?'

'You're in the garden of the Apothecaries Hall. Don't try to sit up for a bit.'

Despite this advice Caroline struggled into a sitting position, although she swooned a little and her whole body felt as if it had been beaten with flails.

'What happened? The last thing I remember is being pummelled and grabbed at. And then I must have lost consciousness because I couldn't breathe.'

Having said this Caroline started shaking, then broke down in uncontrolled tears. Alice held her while she recovered and wiped the tearstains from her face when she stopped. Caroline took a deep breath to recover her composure and then asked again what had happened. As she did so, she became aware that not only was her sister there but also, of all people, Roddy MacDonald, and further off some of his friends. She raised her eyebrows questioningly to her sister, who smiled at her and then at Roddy.

'It was Roddy who saved us. He was inside the grounds of the Hall when he saw what was happening and with the help of his friends wrestled the key from John Common and went into the crowd and pulled you out. I was not in such a difficult position and I was able to follow him to the clear.'

Caroline's mind was still bemused but she turned to Roddy to thank him. 'I am most grateful,l Mr MacDonald. Most grateful. But I see that you've suffered some injuries to your face in the process.'

'Just a scratch, Miss Caroline. Just a scratch. You put up quite a fight.'

Caroline had a sudden memory of hands grabbing at her and her dress and her punching out at the assailant. 'You mean I did that? I'm terribly sorry.'

And Caroline at first did not say any more, because, as her mind cleared, she remembered that part of her panic had been that she had felt she was being assaulted in a sexual way. She flushed then and kept her head low before jerking bolt upright.

'The exam. The exam.'

'Oh, I don't think you should be worrying about the exam after all you've been through.' said Alice.

'Oh no. We must get to the exam.' Caroline struggled to her feet helped by Alice and also by Roddy whose strong hand she was happy to accept.

Alice had mentally written off the exam and had not thought through what the consequences of not sitting would have on the progress of their studies. She was too concerned about the immediate effect on her sister of the ordeal she had gone through. She protested that it was a crazy notion, but Caroline insisted she was not going to let all their hard work go to waste and eventually Alice allowed herself to be persuaded.

She helped Caroline to adjust her dress and put back on her shoes which Roddy had apparently managed to retrieve from where they had been torn from her feet outside. She thanked him with a smile, still a little shy after what had happened and supported on either side by Alice and Roddy, she limped her way to the Hall. On the way, she said to her sister with half a grimace and half a smile,

'We should really be grateful to Miss Clegg and her mania for time-keeping. that we still have the time for this.'

Alice did not respond.

At the Apothecaries Hall they were met by Lucy and Margaret Campbell who had waited outside, anxious because of the delay in their arriving. Alice quickly explained what had happened and, after Caroline assured them that she was fine, they all went in to the Hall.

Once she was safely seated in the examination room Caroline had no further problems. With the concentrated intensity, that had made her father almost in awe of her, she tackled the papers and finished well within the given time. Alice, too, sailed through the assignments with her customary calmness. When she went to Caroline when it was all over, she found that Caroline, having been sitting in the one position for nearly three hours, was so stiff she could hardly move; so that Alice had to assist her to get outside.

Once they got there, however she was delighted to see the large figure of Roddy waiting for them. He had finished his own exam and had anticipated that Alice might need help with Caroline. He was, in fact, going to give help whether Caroline needed it or not but, despite her protestations, she was completely exhausted, now that the stimulus of tackling the exam had been removed.

Roddy called a cab and insisted on accompanying them home. On the way, they naturally discussed what had been in the examination papers, but this very quickly became a dialogue between Alice and Roddy as Caroline found it more and more difficult to concentrate on what was being said. When they arrived Roddy again assisted Alice in getting Caroline from the cab to the Burton's house. Mrs Burton had seen the cab arriving and, wondering why it had come, herself opened the door to find her younger daughter being half carried by her elder daughter and a strange man. Mrs Burton may have seemed frivolous, but she was practical. It took only a few words of explanation that Caroline had become caught up in some mob violence to satisfy her immediate questioning. She summoned Anna and then directed Roddy to wait with Alice in the drawing room while she and Anna took Caroline upstairs. There Anna supervised a hot bath and made sure that Caroline was safely tucked up in bed before she and Mrs Burton came downstairs leaving Caroline already almost asleep.

The drawing room was furnished to Mrs Burton's taste and even her husband found it a little too crowded with delicate things for him to be truly comfortable, preferring the more Spartan surroundings of his study. Roddy, who was considerably bigger than Mr Burton, was a little fearful of sitting down on any of the chairs as he was not sure if they would bear his weight. He passed the time standing looking out of the window at the beautifully laid out gardens and thinking how lucky he was to have been able to give such a personal service to his adored.

When Mrs Burton came in she told him that she had ordered some tea to be brought and meantime asked him to take a chair. Roddy chose what seemed to him to be the stoutest but even then, he sat on the very edge almost trying to keep his weight on his feet. The tea, when it came, was served in a very fine china cup which Roddy handled reverentially, just in case. He took his cue from Alice in playing down the danger Caroline and she had been in and, in any event, was anxious to minimise his whole role in the matter. After he was assured that Caroline was resting and seemed none worst for her ordeal the talk turned to general discussion about the medical course. Then Roddy began to take his leave after first, very carefully, replacing his teacup quite relieved he did not seem to have caused it any damage.

Before he could leave, however, Mr Burton arrived home from his office and the whole story had to be repeated for his benefit. n the town he had heard rumours that a serious riot had taken place although he had had no idea his daughters were caught up in it. While he was worldly wise enough to discount the more exaggerated accounts he had heard, he had a shrewd suspicion that both Alice and Roddy were playing down the seriousness of what had taken place and when he was escorting Roddy to the door he thanked him profusely and said he had shown himself to be a real friend to the family, which would not be forgotten. This was music to Roddy's ears and he walked down the driveway a happy man.

Meantime, as he retired to his study, Mr Burton was determining how he would make sure that the origins of the riot were properly investigated and that those who were responsible made to pay for their actions.

14

The next day Alice went alone to the College as Mrs Burton had insisted that Caroline, despite her protests, should take the day off to recover. Caroline at first had felt totally refreshed. She had slept well, at one stage having a dream that, in a panic, she was being pursued through a forest by a large bear. When to her horror, it caught up with her it changed as is the way of dreams into a warm cosy rug in which she wrapped herself in blissful peace. She slept long and when she did get up she found she was still very stiff. She examined herself in the mirror and found she had large bruises on her inner thigh and on her left breast, which she realised with mounting blushes could only have been caused by Rory's hands when he had grabbed her from the throng. She managed to put this out of her mind while she had breakfast, following which her mother's advice proved well-founded, as she again felt very weak and returned to her bed.

When Alice reached the College, she found the girls full of talk about the exam but, in particular, about the riot. All of them had suffered the abuse of the crowd as they made their way to Apothecaries Hall but most of them had passed through the gates before they had been locked. The morning newspapers were, however filled with reports of what had happened, more or less lurid, depending on the type of newspaper. Their opinion columns followed the tenor of the reports.

The Caledonian denounced what had happened as a disgrace to the city. It reiterated its support for further educational opportunities for women and it called on the city fathers to carry out an in-depth inquiry into what had happened.

The Daily Register pronounced it had long foreseen that something of this sort would occur once this disastrous experiment of women's medical education had been foisted on the good ladies of the city. Those involved in what the Register described as a demonstration, had perhaps gone a little far in showing their opposition but that was merely an indication of the strength of feeling against what was going on.

The leading national paper did not comment on the story until a few days later and when it did so it was to comment that the northern parts of the country still had a little way to go to achieve the level of reasoned debate which was the hallmark of an advanced civilized society.

Miss Clegg, of course, did not read the Daily Register, but she did read the Caledonian's report when she arrived at the College some time before the students started to arrive. She was in the precincts of the Apothecaries Hall before the real trouble broke out, but she had watched it unfold from the distance and had seen Caroline Burton being carried through the gates by some large man, with her sister in attendance. When Mrs Black arrived, she was anxious to discuss things with Miss Clegg, but Miss Clegg did not give a hint of what she was thinking, merely compressing her lips when Mrs Black said that wasn't it typical that the two Burton sisters were in the forefront of the trouble.

The students were unusually excited when Miss Clegg came in to address the morning assembly. She congratulated the girls on having reached what she regarded as a milestone in sitting the examination, which was a public demonstration of the reality of women's medical education. She had no doubt that they would all do well at least as well as their male counterparts.

'And then,' as Alice told Caroline later 'she went to discuss the following week's lectures. She didn't even mention the riot. After she went, we were all left completely puzzled. Some felt that perhaps she had not been there herself, but others confirmed she had been - I saw her myself. It is the oddest thing. All I could think of was that it was some sort of show of strength as if what had happened was one of those things which she had warned us against and which should be ignored in pursuit of our ultimate goal. But it was odd. Almost not human.'

'Yes,' said Caroline. 'More like superhuman. Or maybe she is like myself; unable to show emotion.' And saying this she put on what she thought was a suitably emotionless face.

Alice sighed, 'Oh Caroline, you're shocking. You know how mother hates it when you put on those faces.'

Which was true, as Mrs Burton regarded Caroline's habit of making funny faces as another example of her younger daughter's failure to act as a young lady should. She was happy, however, a little later when Roddy, learning that Caroline had not been at College that day, called to ask after her well-being. Mrs Burton felt that Caroline behaved as perfectly demurely as she could have wished. In truth, Caroline, unusually for her, was a little shy. She was not sure of her emotions. She could still feel the pain from the bruising where Roddy had grabbed her and when she looked at his large, strong hands she experienced a feeling of warmth she could not explain to herself. When she was alone she decided that she rather liked the feeling; she welcomed it when it returned - whenever she thought of Roddy's hands.

Subsequently Caroline and Alice saw Roddy nearly every day as they made their way to the College. She had a sense of disappointment if occasionally Roddy failed to appear, and she and Alice would linger to see if he would turn up. This had the knock-on effect of making them late for registration, much to Mrs Black's unconcealed displeasure. Alice had little time for Mrs Black or her views, but it is a funny aspect of human nature that our self-esteem depends on the opinions of others, even those whom we regard as fools, and she always felt a little put out whenever Mrs Black made quite clear her antagonism. The ill-feeling between the sisters and Mrs Black was the one major black spot on the sisters' enjoyment of their studies. Because of the situation of her office they felt she was constantly watching them like a spy and no doubt reporting back to Miss Clegg any perceived breach of behaviour.

The meetings with Roddy were still tacitly considered as accidental, no matter how regularly they took place. If Roddy had had a sister he might have learnt from her how to ingratiate himself into a girl's feelings with a little flattery, a few comments about how well she was looking and perhaps some compliments about the dress she was wearing. But Roddy did not have a sister - although Lucy might have filled the gap. That, though, would have meant Roddy explaining his feelings to Lucy and he could not have brought himself to express these publicly. Even if he had this advice, in truth Roddy could not have put it into practice. He did like the way Caroline looked and the way she dressed but he just could not see himself paying any of these little courtesies without tying himself in knots. And so, he confined himself to chatting about the courses they were taking.

Caroline, of course, did have a sister and when Alice sensed what was happening she tried to manoeuvre things so that the young lovers, as she saw them, could have short periods on their own. Caroline, however, soon sensed what was happening and told her sister not to be silly, as she was perfectly happy and indeed preferred it when the three of them were together.

Roddy was on surer ground when talking about medical matters. Although it was never mentioned, the sisters were aware of a rumour that Roddy had come top of the exam they had all taken. They were surprised, however, when he said that his favourite class was Materia Medica.

'We all hate it,' said Alice. 'At least everyone apart from Lucy. Poor Dr Boring. I think that, having lost her father, she's attending to Dr Boring the way she would have done towards him. It's quite sweet. But the rest of us... Why on earth are you so keen?'

Roddy shrugged. 'I think it's because at home I was interested in plants and flowers. And almost everything they are now discovering is based on preparations derived from nature. You know when you are stung by a nettle you can get relief from the pain, by rubbing with a leaf from a docken which is always growing nearby. That is because, just as there is something in the nettle which causes the sting, there is some substance in the docken which has pain relieving qualities. And it is clear, that other plants and trees will have similar qualities which are just waiting to be discovered. That is what I find so exciting.'

The sisters, being well brought-up city girls, had never been involved in rubbing nettle stings with docken leaves, but his enthusiasm was infectious, and they were happy to let him ramble on about what he hoped to do in the future. Caroline, by this time, had forgotten she had ever imagined he spoke only to his sheep. Her new fantasy, she told Alice, was that she saw him wandering amongst the fields with flowers in his hair.

15

The Colonial Infirmary

29 October

Dear Miss Clegg,

I regret to have to write to you but the actions of four of your students leave me with no choice.

As you know the arrangements made between the College and the Infirmary permit the students access to the surgical wards between 3 and 5 each weekday. There was originally a little difficulty about sticking to these times, but it was made plain to the students that the timetable must be adhered to, so as to avoid interference with the smooth running of the hospital.

I was therefore most surprised this afternoon, when making my rounds, to find the four students still in the wards at 5.20. When I told them to leave, I was treated with great rudeness by Miss Alice Burton, who seemed to be the ringleader, and I was told that it was not my position to interfere with the arrangements which had been made for them by the House Surgeon. A rather unpleasant scene then ensued before the four took their leave.

I am writing to you rather than raising the matter formally with the Infirmary authorities in the hope that you will be able to discipline those involved who were Miss Alice Burton, Miss Caroline Burton, Miss Edith Smith and Miss Anne MacTavish.

Yours sincerely,
Elizabeth Murdoch
Infirmary Superintendent

The College for the Education and Promotion of Ladies in Medicine

30 October

Dear Miss Murdoch,

I was greatly upset to receive your letter. It was bad enough that the students concerned should break the rules clearly laid down but intolerable that they should compound their misdemeanour by disputing your authority to enforce them.

I have ordered the students concerned to send you a letter of apology which I trust you will find acceptable.

I regret that you have been troubled in this way.

Yours sincerely,

Jennifer Clegg,

Dean

The College for the Education and Promotion of Ladies in Medicine

30 October

Dear Miss Murdoch,

We beg to apologise to you for our breach last Tuesday of the regulations laid down by the Infirmary for access to the surgical wards and the manner in which one of our number spoke to you at that occasion.

We assure that no such further misconduct by us will take place.

We are yours obediently,

Alice Burton
Caroline Burton
Edith Smith
Anne MacTavish

The College for the Education and Promotion of Ladies in Medicine

1 November

Dear Miss Murdoch,

I wish to withdraw the apology sent to you yesterday. It was prepared by Miss Clegg and as soon as it was sent I regretted having signed it.

I am sure that you find it as unpleasant to receive a forced apology as it was for me to sign it.

I regret that our absorption in the treatment being given to the injured patient by the House Surgeon made us overlook the hospital regulations which are your province. I regret that this may have caused offence.

Yours sincerely,

Alice Burton

The Caledonian Infirmary

2 November

Dear Miss Clegg,

On Monday, I received a letter of apology signed by the four students involved in the recent nastiness and regarded the matter to be at an end. But then yesterday I received the enclosed further letter from Miss Alice Burton.

I am too busy to be involved in further correspondence in this regard and should be most grateful if on your part, you would endeavour to impose some discipline on the students under your jurisdiction.

This apart I value our continued cooperation in providing opportunities for the young ladies which I hope will not have to be withdrawn.

Yours sincerely,

Elizabeth Murdoch

The Colonial Infirmary lay on the outskirts of the city. When Miss Clegg was making the preparations for the establishment of her College, it was essential that the prospective students had access to hospital wards in order that they could observe patients in an active environment. However, the main city hospital, a bastion of male opposition to her plans, was not prepared to afford her the required facilities and it was only after much work and persuasion that she had been able to make the necessary arrangements with the Colonial Infirmary which did not have the same standing nor the same antipathy.

The Infirmary was so called because its establishment had been funded by expatriates who had made their fortunes in the colonies. It had fairly recently been built in the modern pavilion fashion, with wings of high-roofed wards lit by large windows on either side to facilitate the circulation of air. It had originally been conceived as a specialist hospital dealing with infectious diseases deriving from the tropics but had developed over time into a more general hospital.

The students called the infirmary **'the Colony'** for short and this was more appropriate than they imagined, because it stood on the site of a former leper colony built there in medieval times when the perceived way of dealing with lepers was to isolate them in communities out with city boundaries.

The students looked forward to their visits to the Colony, for which they were organised into small groups. The only drawback was the inflexibility of the infirmary's insistence on the hours of access; frequently a visit coincided with a period when nothing of interest was happening only for a fascinating case to come in towards the end the designated time. To the girls, it seemed another example of regulations being imposed just for the sake of uniformity. The difficulty was that at the Colony end, arrangements were in the hands of the Lady Superintendent who, in the fine tradition of matrons, believed in a hospital run on strict disciplinary lines. To be fair to the Lady Superintendent the students, when left to their own devices, tended to become lax especially in their arrival times and there had been occasional reprimands because of this.

On the day in question the group of girls was just about to leave when they ran into the House Surgeon who invited them to see an extremely rare case which had just come in. His enthusiasm was infectious, and they followed him into the ward where, as any young man would, he delighted in displaying his knowledge before four young ladies who showed their appreciation of his expertise. In particular, he identified Alice as someone who appreciated right away what he was trying to achieve, and he found himself discussing matters with her as he would have done with a colleague. While this was going on, Miss Murdoch came into the ward and demanded to know what was happening. The surgeon explained that the girls were there on his invitation, but Miss Murdoch cut short his explanation, took the girls aside and told them to leave immediately.

Alice was annoyed not only by losing their chance to see the case but also by the peremptory way in which they were addressed and spoke out accordingly, 'I should have thought that in these matters the permission of a medical practitioner should over-ride the requirements of non-professional staff.'

Miss Murdoch drew herself up to her full height (which was not very great and much below that of Alice). 'I am not interested in your opinion, Miss. I am in charge of the arrangements for your visit. You will leave immediately.'

Alice, angered by what she saw as unnecessary interference, now became flushed and retorted that their medical education was a more important thing than the running of the hospital.

Both she and Miss Murdoch would have pursued the dispute further but Caroline, of all people, was the coolest headed of all those involved, and she managed to pull her sister away from the conflict and out of the premises. However, Alice was still complaining about the stupidity of the rules and the pig-headedness of Miss Murdoch all the way back to the College.

Alice had calmed down by the next day when the students gathered for the Assembly. The news of the altercation had become known to all the girls - who had all had similar problems at the Colony. It was just one more of the restrictions under which they chafed.

When Miss Clegg came in, her expression was severe, but the girls did not pick up any difference to her normal demeanour. She held a piece of paper in her hand.

'I have just received this letter of complaint from the Lady Superintendent. It states that, despite often repeated instructions, four members of the class remained at the Colonial Infirmary beyond the permitted time and then disputed the Lady Superintendent's authority to enforce the agreed rules. The persons concerned are named as Miss Alice Burton, Miss Caroline Burton, Miss Edith Smith, and Miss Anne MacTavish. Would the persons named stand and give an account of themselves.'

Somewhat reluctantly the four girls rose to their feet.

As the other three looked at her, Alice took the responsibility of speaking. 'What has been said is broadly speaking true but - '

Miss Clegg interrupted. 'Don't shilly-shally with me, Miss. Are the allegations true?'

'I was trying to explain that we stayed on at the express invitation of the House Surgeon and - '

'I am not aware that the House Surgeon has any right to interfere with the way I organise this College, nor could his intervention justify you in insulting the Lady Superintendent, who has authority over you when you are in the Infirmary premises.'

Alice had to accept that there was much truth in Miss Clegg's attack; it just wasn't the whole story. And she didn't know how to respond.

'You have brought the good name of the College into disrepute. As it is clear that none of you know how to behave properly in a professional situation, I have prepared a letter of apology which Mrs Black will have you sign. In addition, your hospital visiting rights will be suspended for one week. Now sit down.'

With that Miss Clegg left the room.

After she left there was considerable hubbub in the room, only brought to an end when Mrs Black told the four girls to accompany to her office to sign the letter of apology. Alice complied with the others although she was still shaken by the way Miss Clegg had dealt with the matter. Mrs Black, on the other hand took considerable satisfaction in seeing her chief adversaries taken down a peg.

'Ye'll no' be sweepin' past me quite so proudly now,' she thought to herself.

As Alice and Caroline went home later that day Caroline, who was never down for long, had decided to put the affair behind her and thought she had persuaded her sister to do likewise. But Alice had a strong sense of justice (or maybe a strong sense of her own worth – they are often the same thing) and she bitterly regretted having signed the letter of apology prepared by Miss Clegg. Without telling Caroline she sent a further letter to Miss Murdoch withdrawing the previous one and expressing her regrets in her own words. Alice was quite proud of her second letter over which she spent much time. It was, however, one of those letters which give much pleasure in composition but should not be sent.

When Miss Clegg saw the second letter, which had been forwarded to her by Miss Murdoch, she was incandescent with rage. By chance, on the morning she received the letter, she was having one of her regular monthly meetings with the Chairman of the Trustees and she told him that Alice's conduct was intolerable; it put at risk the continuing operation of the College and she ought to be expelled from the

College. The Chairman, Mr Bryden, was a local minister and was well aware that his function and the function of the Board generally was to agree with whatever decisions Miss Clegg came to. But despite Miss Clegg's low opinion of him he had years of experience in dealing with difficult parishioners. He detected in Miss Clegg's use of the word 'ought' that she was not totally determined to proceed with expulsion and by use of profuse expressions of sympathy he managed to secure her agreement that, if a further direct apology was made, the matter could be dealt with by increasing the punishment to two weeks' suspension of access to the Colony.

The next day at Assembly, as Alice had rather feared, Miss Clegg told her to stand. Her heart sank as she recognised in Miss Clegg's hand the letter she had sent to Miss Murdoch.

'I understand from Miss Murdoch that despite my instructions you have gone against my expressed wishes in this sorry matter. This is not the first time you have presumed to challenge my running of this College. I will not have it. If you are unhappy with the way we do things, you are free to withdraw. It is up to you. I will be leaving in half an hour to visit Miss Murdoch to express my regrets face to face. If you wish to remain in this College you will accompany me. Please let me know your decision through Mrs Black. If you are to remain, your visiting rights suspension will be increased to two weeks.'

With that she strode from the room.

The students sat in stunned silence for a moment then gradually left without speaking to Alice, although Margaret Campbell patted her shoulder as she passed. Caroline remained with her sister and made as if to speak but Alice shook her head and Caroline, too, left the room but not before kissing her sister as she went.

Alone, Alice paced up and down with her hands behind her back. Her first reaction was anger - no, fury. She had been humiliated before the whole class and now was expected to be dragged up by Miss Clegg like a naughty schoolchild to abase herself before Mrs Murdoch. She was just not prepared to do that. We Burtons have our pride, she thought. But that very thought brought to mind her father. What would he do? The first thing he would have counselled was to keep calm and, as he had taught her, she forced herself to slow down and deepen her breathing.

She remembered a saying of his. 'Don't let your mistakes dictate your decisions.' Had she made mistakes? **Yes**. In staying outwith the permitted hours? **Yes.** In challenging the authority of Miss Murdoch? **Yes**. In sending that silly second letter which was just a sop to her pride? **Yes**. Was she going to make yet another mistake in destroying her dreams of a medical career, and possibly those of her sister, because of misplaced pride? No, no, no.

As she sat in the carriage with Miss Clegg, neither saying a word, Alice felt almost serene. Her imperfections had been publicly exposed, but it was only foolish pride that made her think that she didn't have any. She felt the stronger for what she had gone through. And when they met Miss Murdoch that good lady could not have been more kind and understanding.

Needless to say, in the carriage on the way back to the College, still not a word passed between Alice and Miss Clegg.

16

Repercussions about the riot were still rumbling on. The Caledonian used it as a vehicle to pursue the Council for its perceived failings generally. More specifically Miss Clegg, tireless in defence of her students, pestered the Council leaders to carry out an investigation into what had happened. Possibly more potently, Mr Burton through his business connections, put pressure on the Council to find an explanation as to why his two daughters had been placed in such danger in broad daylight on the public streets of the city.

Eventually, as is often the case, the Council leaders decided that it was less trouble to have an enquiry rather than fight off continued criticism and a date was fixed for the matter to be aired at a meeting of the Council early the following month. Miss Clegg was invited to be present.

Miss Clegg had been in the City Chambers on a number of occasions and although she was nervous, she was not overawed by the splendour of the building. But Mrs Black, who was with her, was wide-eyed at the size of the building, which had a commanding position fronting a large square; and even more so as she climbed the sweeping staircase lined with marble which led up to the Council Chamber itself, on the first floor. The Chamber was a grand room hung with chandeliers from the high ornate ceiling, with portraits of former Provosts on the walls and with highly polished wood tables and chairs for the Councillors. At one end, there was a raised area with a finely carved desk at which sat the Council Leader and his staff. The Chamber was capable of accommodating about a hundred people and Miss Clegg was disappointed to find that it was less than half full; of course, all those present were men. As a well-known figure in the town she was welcomed by name by the Council leader, Baillie Clark but he asked who her companion was. Miss Clegg introduced Mrs Black as her Secretary and explained she had come as moral support.

Baillie Clark said, with his most disarming smile, 'But I assure you that that is scarcely necessary. We are all friends here.'

After so many years of struggle Miss Clegg was impervious to disarming smiles, but she bowed in acknowledgement. As she looked around the chamber she was disconcerted to note that not only was it less than half full, but one councillor was reading a newspaper and three others were engaged in a lively discussion over some documents spread out before them, which had obviously nothing to do with the enquiry. She was even more dismayed when some of those in the chamber left obviously on more pressing business, and others wandered in who had missed previous discussions.

Baillie Clark asked the Council Officer to give an account of his investigations.

'On the morning of the fourteenth of October, the Constabulary reports that the city streets near the University area were unusually busy. The reason for this was either the weekly market or some general curiosity following a report in the Daily Register that the ladies who were studying in the Ladies Medical College would be passing that way to sit an examination at the Apothecaries Hall.

'The students, when they emerged as a group from the College, were readily identifiable and were followed by an increasing crowd included in which were some who were totally opposed to the whole idea of women's medical training. It would appear that those who were in opposition, many of whom were women of the lower classes, took the opportunity of their proximity to the students to vent their feelings in a more vehement way than was possibly justifiable. A greater crush then developed when the ladies turned into Apothecaries Lane which, as you know, is narrower than the main thoroughfare. Most of the students, despite this, were able to make their way into the grounds of the Apothecaries Hall. Unfortunately, through a misunderstanding, the gate into the Apothecary Hall grounds was locked prematurely leaving several of the students marooned outside. The stranded students were then subjected to the increasing pressure of the crowd until it was found possible to re-open the gate and let them through.

'Thereafter I understand that all the students were able to pass into the Apothecaries Hall and sit their examination.'

Baillie Clark thanked the Council Officer and said, 'I think that is a very fair narration of what took place and it has certainly clarified for me a number of things which I had not previously understood. Unless Miss Clegg has any comments to add I propose that we accept the Council Officer's Report and then move on to other business.'

Miss Clegg slowly rose to her feet. During the reading of the Report she had become increasingly agitated and now she had to tell herself to keep calm and not to let her feelings run away from her. She was totally unprepared for the terms of the Report and could not believe how it glossed over the events of that day. Her voice was normally severe but now it came out louder and harsher as she tried to make herself heard in the cavernous chamber. In addition, by nature she bludgeoned people rather than tried to persuade them and she could not change now.

'Baillie Clark that Report is a disgrace.'

This created uproar in the Chamber and even those councillors who had up till now shown no interest in the proceedings turned to her.

'On the morning in question there were no constables to be seen at any stage. More's the pity. In addition, you should be aware, if you ever have attended the market, that any crowds drawn to it would long since have departed before the emergence of my students from the College.

'No. The sole reason for the crowd was the campaign whipped up by the Daily Register, which almost spurred on people to turn up and, if not to prevent the students' progress, to make that progress as unpleasant as possible.'

One Councillor, tightly trussed into his 'Meeting' suit rose to speak through the chair. 'Baillie, Miss Clegg may not agree with the views expressed by the Daily Register, but they reflect the opinion of many people including quite a few in this chamber and including, I may say, many in the medical profession.'

Miss Clegg turned to him. 'The Daily Register is entitled to express its views, but it ought to have a sense of responsibility in exercising that right. To incite disruption which it should have known could lead to verbal and physical abuse is conduct verging on a crime.' Miss Clegg thereafter remained on her feet as interjections came in from all over the chamber, increasingly ignoring the formality of addressing the comments through the chair.

To a rumble of approval another Councillor interjected. 'I understand from the Council Officer's Report that all the young ladies were able to proceed to sit the examination, which would suggest that we are talking about a minor disturbance which was speedily overcome. Many of us do feel that one drawback to the medical teaching of women is that they are not suited to the rough and tumble which is inseparable from actual medical practice. I feel that this experience proves our point.'

Miss Clegg pursed her lips. 'You do a great disservice to the students involved. That they were able to proceed with the examination does not minimise the ordeal they suffered; that they went ahead despite the trauma they had experienced is a tribute to their courage and resilience. As someone who has experience of medical practice I can assure you, Councillor, that many men would have used the riot as an excuse for missing the examination.'

Another Councillor the very Baillie Macnair who had originally agreed to be a Trustee before withdrawing at the last minute, then made the fundamental mistake of asking a question without knowing the answer. 'Miss Clegg appears to know so much more than anyone else whom the Council Officer questioned. What I would like to know is how she knows so much. Was she actually there at the time?'

Miss Clegg snapped back. 'Of course, I was there. (The words 'you fool' were not stated but were understood by everyone in the chamber). I was there throughout. Despite this, the Council Officer in his 'investigation' chose not to speak to me nor, as far as I know, to any of the students. It would suggest a less than thorough approach.'

Baillie Clark intervened. 'Miss Clegg, I don't think there is any need to attack a council official who has left the chamber and in any event who is not entitled to speak in this forum.'

The mood in the Chamber had now changed. Those who had attended originally, had expected a routine Council Report which would have been sufficient to ward off any criticism of the Council's inactivity. They regarded Miss Clegg's presence as purely formal expecting her to accept the Report submissively in gratitude to the Council for going to such length. But their concept of feminine docility in the face of superior masculine understanding of public affairs was being challenged; not just challenged but rigorously denied. And they did not like it. Their initial pose of courtesy towards a weak woman was replaced by resentment at her audacity in resisting what they saw as the will of the Council. Even those who had seen the situation as an opportunity to attack their political opponents were now united with these opponents in assailing Miss Clegg.

By this time, too, news had spread around the City Chambers that something was happening in the Chamber and it began to fill up. Comments came from all over the Chamber and were increasingly greeted with shouts of approval while Miss Clegg's responses were uniformly met with cries of dissent. And Baillie Clark had long since given up any attempt to keep order.

A newly arrived Councillor intervened. 'It seems to me that all that took place was that members of the lower classes expressed, in public, in their rough way, views on this educational experiment which many of us in this chamber share and would not be unwilling to state now.'

Miss Clegg turned to him, 'That may be true, but I would not expect you to express these views accompanied by oaths and vile comments, coupled with spitting and attempted assaults. You taint yourself by association, Councillor.'

The Councillor responded angrily. 'I think that we should be looking at the root cause of the stramash. I don't think that even Miss Clegg would deny that if there had been no Ladies Medical College there would have been no trouble. The Ladies accordingly would seem to have brought this on their own heads.'

Miss Clegg shook her head in frustration. 'If that is true, Councillor, I trust you will reflect on your own foolishness in having possessions, the next time a burglar breaks into your house. My students were subjected throughout to a torrent of abuse which, once they turned into Apothecaries Lane, developed into physical violence threatening severe injury to them when it was discovered that the gates to the Hall had been closed against them.'

'Now, now, Miss Clegg.' Baillie Clark smiled placatingly, 'I think we all realise that a difficult situation was made worse by the misunderstanding which resulted in the locking of the gate.'

Miss Clegg glared at him. 'This was not a 'difficult situation' as you call it. This was not a crowd. It was not a mob. It was a riot. And there was no misunderstanding. The locking of the gate was done deliberately by male students who, despite the early hour, seem to have been under the influence of alcohol and -'

She was interrupted before she could go further by cries of protest and shame from many of the Councillors.

Baillie Clark frowned. 'Miss Clegg, I must ask you to withdraw that last statement immediately. You must be aware from the reaction that it has caused offence to Councillors some of whom have connections with the students involved. It is totally wrong to make accusations against fine young men who are not here to defend themselves.'

Miss Clegg stood alone amidst the now crowded Chamber, her voice becoming even louder as she strove to make herself heard above the tumult. 'If you wish I will withdraw the comment. In making it, I was trying to find an excuse for the loutish behaviour of those concerned. Very well then, the students were not intoxicated. They were perfectly sober when they perpetrated actions which were a disgrace to this city and their university and which could have led to the severe injury if not the death of some of my students.'

'Baillie Clark, 'Another Councillor shouted from his seat, 'I think Miss Craig, Oh I am sorry, Miss **Clegg**, is harming whatever case she is making by overstating it. After all no damage appears to have suffered apart, no doubt, from some minor displacement of dress which would be easily rectified. And is it not the case that the same students, when they saw the predicament the young ladies were in, opened the gate and came to their rescue?'

Miss Clegg threw up her hands and almost wearily responded. 'Yes, some of the male students came to their aid but it was not the same students.'

'At least you are not maligning the whole student body,' a further Councillor spoke, as he thought, magnanimously. 'This seems to me to be just an example of youthful high spirits which at our stage in life we deplore but which we all suffered from when we were younger.'

One of his colleagues shouted from behind Miss Clegg, 'I agree. It is a storm in a teacup which some newspapers have exaggerated for their own ends.'

A little fat Councillor rose to say sardonically, 'The whole matter arises when parties with their own agenda try to push themselves into areas where they are not wanted. Where is it all going to end? Are we going to end up with woman ministers in the Kirk?'

This caused some general merriment with various councillors exchanging jibes before Baillie Clark called for order.

'I think you will agree gentlemen that we have discussed this matter adequately. With your approval, I will inform the Constabulary that a greater presence may be required on future occasions and perhaps, Miss Clegg, you would be good enough to liaise with them whenever the occasion warrants.

'We shall now pass on to further business. Miss Clegg, you may remain if you wish but you might prefer to withdraw at this stage. Thank you for your attendance today.'

Without acknowledging the Baillie, Miss Clegg rose to her feet and strode out of the chamber with Mrs Black in her wake. As she left the room she was aware that there was an immediate hubbub amongst the Councillors who remained.

You can only batter against a brick wall for so long and Miss Clegg felt a momentary weariness before firming her spirits again. Mrs Black, for her part, longed to tell Miss Clegg how well she had done but she knew that Miss Clegg would not have welcomed any such comment from her. Mrs Black felt that Miss Clegg had been like one of the early Christians she had read about who were put to death in the Roman Circus. Mrs Black had always thought that the Romans had funny ideas as to what they wanted in their circuses but, that apart, she felt proud when she thought how Miss Clegg had stood alone while being attacked from all sides. If only those silly girls at the College had seen her they might have a greater appreciation of her true worth.

17

Towards the end of the term Lucy received a pleasant surprise in the post. It was her Education Certificate, which the examiners informed her had been issued after reappraisal of the two papers on which she had fallen down in the previous year's exam. It was a surprise and also a relief because it meant she neither had to spend time studying the subjects concerned nor worry that she might fail yet again, thereby ending her hopes of a medical career.

When she reached the College the first person she sought out was Dr Ring because it was to him, rather than her friends, she had confided her concerns about the exam. He was delighted with her news and congratulated her that she could now concentrate on her current studies without having this re- sit hanging over her.

She then told her two friends, Alice and Caroline, and admitted to them for the first time that she had been worried the whole term about how she would do in re-sitting the exam. Alice gave her a good scolding for not have shared her worries before this because the two sisters had noticed that Lucy had become quieter and had wondered at the reason.

'Let's do something to celebrate,' said Caroline. 'You know that lovely walk to Praxton? The weather is going to be good, so we could go there on Saturday and take a picnic with us.'

'It's a long way to go on our own,' said the more practical Alice.

'There's no problem' responded Caroline. 'Lucy, you contact Roddy and see if he is up for it. And we could ask Margaret if she wants to come as well.'

It turned out that Margaret had arranged to go home that weekend but Roddy quickly shelved the plans he had for the Saturday. Arrangements were accordingly made and there was great excitement in the preparations. Roddy was to pick up Lucy from her house and bring her to the Burton's house, their point of departure.

When Saturday dawned, it promised to be a beautiful day but when Roddy arrived it was without Lucy. When he had called at her house he was told by her mother that she had been unwell overnight and couldn't come; she insisted they went ahead in her absence.

Anna prepared the picnic and made sure that the girls were suitably dressed for the day. The two girls set off with Roddy who was carrying, not only his own modest requirements for the day, but also a considerable extra load of things the sisters regarded as essential to their enjoyment of the walk. His burden was added to as the day went on, as the sisters gradually discarded extra clothing which they had donned as a precaution against the early morning cool.

There was a direct road to the village of Praxton but, shortly after they were clear of the town, they branched off to take a grassy path which gave them a more attractive route through woods and open fields. As they meandered along, the girls were astonished once again at Roddy's knowledge of the flowers and the countryside. Now that he was more at ease with them, he spoke more confidently, sharing his knowledge without giving any impression that he was showing off. The woods were full of the sounds of birds and he was able to distinguish the different songs for their benefit. At one stage when they were walking near a stream he motioned them to hush and as they moved forward carefully he pointed out a kingfisher swooping down for fish in the water.

They had almost reached the village when they decided that as it was such a lovely day they would not go on to the village for their picnic but have it where they were, which was a little glade beside the stream with good cover from the sun for the benefit of the girls. By this time, Roddy was desperate to relieve himself and he made the excuse of collecting some water so that he could go deeper into the woods for this purpose. It did not occur to him for a second that the girls might have a similar need, but they took advantage of his absence to make themselves comfortable.

They then set out the picnic things and on his return Roddy took pleasure in seeing them working together arranging things neatly in ways that suited them. It had been agreed that the girls would provide (although not carry) the picnic and the sandwiches and pies and cakes were all beautifully prepared. It occurred to Roddy that, had the food preparation been left to him, it might have looked less appetising but possibly more filling. However, although at first, he restrained himself so as not to eat more than he should, there was easily enough for all of them and they ate their fill. Afterwards they talked lazily as they relaxed in the sun mostly, as might be imagined, about the College and their fellow students. Roddy was curious to know more about Miss Clegg, but Caroline declared that it was too nice a day to spoil with thinking about her and Black Bob.

After a while Roddy announced that the day was getting on and that they should start back. Before they set off, they all helped in gathering the picnic things and in tidying up where they had been sitting. They had only gone less than fifty yards before Caroline gave a sharp cry and fell to the ground. She had caught her foot on a hidden root and, although she had not hurt herself in her fall, she was obviously in great pain from where she had twisted her ankle.

With Caroline still on the ground they discussed what they should do. Alice remembered that on their walk they had passed a small cottage which was now only two or three hundred yards away and Roddy set off to see if they could get assistance there. He reported back that there was someone there, a lady who could not have been more helpful, and who was happy for them to rest there to see whatever further arrangements could be made.

Alice and Roddy were able to get Caroline up on her feet and supporting her on either side, they made their way to the cottage, a small single-storey building containing two rooms, one a living room with a fire in the grate which, despite the summer weather was lit, and a room off, which was used as a bedroom. The lady of the house, Mrs Gibson, fussed round Caroline and insisted that she make herself comfortable on the bed. While they were doing this Roddy returned and gathered up the belongings they had had to leave behind. When he got back to the cottage he found that Mrs Gibson had already set out some cups and a kettle was on the range for a pot of tea.

While he had been away Alice and Mrs Gibson had obviously been discussing the next step. It appeared that in Praxton village there was a man who had a pony and trap who could take them back home. Mrs Gibson had a son who had hidden himself away, staring out at these strange people who had invaded his home. Mrs Gibson sent the boy to fetch the trap owner, with strict instructions to go straight there; and off he went. As could be imagined there was a difference in interpretation between mother and son as to what 'straight there' meant. In the boy's case, it involved jumping over the stream at various points to see how far he could jump; this included some splashy failures but that is one advantage of not wearing shoes. As well as jumping, the journey involved racing some sticks along the same stream, climbing a favourite tree, and checking a snare to see if anything had been caught. (Nothing had ever been caught but the snare had always to be inspected just in case). There was, as a result, some delay in the boy reaching the trap owner's house and even more before the pony and trap arrived back at the cottage with the boy proudly ensconced on the front bench beside the driver.

Meanwhile, Alice having removed Caroline's stocking was trying to decide how bad the damaged ankle was.

'Get Roddy in to see it,' said Caroline. 'He'll know.'

'Oh, that would scarcely be proper,' replied Alice.

'Don't be silly, Alice. He's our friend. He won't mind.'

'I'm sure he wouldn't,' said Alice. That's not quite the point.'

But eventually, over her protests, Caroline called to Roddy to come in and inspect the stricken ankle. Now it must be remembered that this was in Victorian times when the sight of a lady's stockinged ankle as she stepped from a carriage was the height of male erotic stimulation. Roddy was thus more than a little tentative when he came into the bedroom and his mouth was dry when Caroline asked him to take a close look at her ankle. He went as near as he dared and said that there didn't seem to be too much damage.

Then Caroline said, 'I've just remembered, Alice. When we were studying anatomy, Miss Clegg said that when you were looking for injury in limbs you should always look at the undamaged limb for comparison.'

And before Alice could stop her she had stripped off the other stocking and presented both bare ankles for Roddy's inspection. While this manoeuvre was going on Roddy was turning the same high shade of red as he had done when he had first offered Caroline his seat on the tram. He managed to control himself by persuading himself that this was the type of thing he would have to get used to as a doctor and he even went as far as touching the injured foot to test for puffiness. Then he had a sudden thought and leaving the bedroom he rummaged through the picnic things, returning with a napkin which he carefully folded and then used as a bandage to dress and support the injured ankle. When he had finished he carefully eased the stocking back over the foot and the bandaged ankle, at which stage Alice jumped in and said that she would take over from there and Roddy left the bedroom with his mind in a whirl at what he had seen and just done.

If Caroline was being honest with herself (which she wasn't, at least not till later) she rather enjoyed sitting back on the bed with her bare ankles exposed to Roddy's gaze and feeling his hands on her leg as he tied the bandage. Alice was still shocked, and she determined that as soon as she had her sister alone she would have strong word with her about her behaviour. She was, however, impressed by the neat way Roddy had bandaged up the ankle.

A short time later the man with the pony and trap arrived and Caroline was helped into it with Alice. When they were made comfortable Roddy said that there wasn't really room for him also and, if they would take the picnic things, he was quite happy to make his own way back to the town. Despite the girls' protestations this was what was done.

After they had gone Roddy tried to make some payment to Mrs Gibson in return for her hospitality, but she refused point blank and said she would be insulted if he persisted. He managed to get round her by suggesting a small payment for the boy for his efforts and this was gratefully accepted. As he left she expressed her best wishes for the young lady's swift recovery and said they must call in again if they were passing.

In the pony and trap Alice, keeping her voice low so as not to be overheard by the driver, scolded Caroline for what Alice thought was her sister's indecorous conduct.

She hoped that Caroline was taking on board her advice, although she said nothing in reply. They sat in silence as the trap rolled along and then Caroline started giggling.

When Alice asked her why she was laughing she replied, 'I was just thinking that, what with pulling me out of the crowd at the Apothecaries Hall, half carrying me to the cottage, and then bandaging my ankle, Roddy has had more hands on my body than anyone else, apart from Mother, since I was a baby.'

'How can you think such a thing, far less say it? Caroline, you are totally incorrigible. ' Alice was really scandalised.

Caroline was inclined to agree but she kept her peace (and her further thoughts) to herself.

Meanwhile Roddy was striding home along the path. He felt absolutely no weariness. he had just spent the happiest few hours of his life. A man of Roddy's bulk was not ideally built for skipping but his step was bouncy as he went along and an occasional loose stone received a hearty kick. He smiled when he remembered Alice's compliments on his neat bandaging. He had not thought it necessary to tell her that in his home village he often spent time at the local stable and had developed his skill, in binding, when required, the fetlocks of the horses.

18

The Monday after the Saturday walk was the final day of the term and both Lucy and Caroline felt sufficiently recovered from their ailments to attend. When Lucy presented herself at registration Mrs Black told her that Miss Clegg wanted to see her.

Lucy had no idea why this should be so. She had been in no trouble during the term, she was a good timekeeper, and she had done reasonably well in the examinations - not as well as the Burton sisters, of course, but they were exceptional. No, there was nothing she could think of. Despite this she was nervous as she stood before the door of Miss Clegg's study. She checked her dress and patted her hair and then putting on her most winning expression, she knocked on the door.

When she went in Miss Clegg was seated at her desk but, as was her wont, she did not ask Lucy to take a seat.

'I am making preparations for next term. Now, you were permitted to attend this term although you did not have the required Certificate of Education. That will not apply next term. When are you due to re-sit the necessary papers?'

'Oh, I don't have to, Miss Clegg,' said Lucy. 'Just last week I received a letter from the examiners enclosing my Certificate and stating that they had re-examined my papers and had decided to upgrade the two which I had failed.'

Miss Clegg's reaction was not what Lucy had anticipated. 'How on earth can that be? On what possible basis did you approach the examiners to re-view your papers?'

'I didn't approach them at all,' said Lucy beginning to feel increasingly nervous at Miss Clegg's response.

'Nonsense, girl. Do you expect me to believe that the examiners, without being asked, took it on themselves to re-examine the year-old papers of someone who was a complete stranger to them? For you to make such an application to them is heinous in itself but for you now to lie about it makes the offence even greater.'

Lucy was by now totally shaken and almost in tears but, when she tried to speak again, she was shut off by Miss Clegg who ordered her to re-join the other students while she decided what action she would take.

After she had left, Miss Clegg remained sitting at her desk, which was as usual completely clear apart from the little box which Miss Clegg stroked as she considered what to do. She had come into the College that morning with the beginnings of a headache which threatened now to get worse. Lucy was the type of woman whom Miss Clegg despised. Someone who would feign helplessness and seek assistance without saying anything, by giving one of her smiles which cried out, 'I am just a poor little thing who needs someone who has the strength I lack to come to my aid.' In Miss Clegg's view, it was a smile which combined weakness with admiration of the recipient's strength. It was the type of smile, she thought, which had condemned women for centuries to a subservient position. With that attitude, women would never ever attain the proper sphere in life which was their right.

And then, having been caught out, not to have the courage to own up to the offence! Just more weakness.

Lucy, meanwhile, had re-joined the other students. She would have preferred to go somewhere first to compose herself but that was not possible given the layout of the College. When they saw how upset she was, they immediately crowded round and gradually, between stifled sobs, she explained what had happened. The girls were totally flabbergasted at Miss Clegg's reaction to the news of Lucy's Certificate.

'Remember how delighted we were when we heard', said Caroline. 'What difference does it make why the examiners decided to change their minds? The important thing is that Lucy has her Certificate and she can keep going with her studies.'

'One thing is absolutely certain,' said Alice. 'If Lucy says she did not approach the examiners, it is outrageous to doubt her word.'

The discussions would have continued but the last Materia Medica lecture of the term was due and the girls started to move off to the lecture hall, with Lucy by now in slightly better control of her feelings. In fact, Dr Ring, as usual concentrating merely on getting through the lecture, would not have noticed anything different was it not for the fact that, throughout the term, Lucy had always come in early to assist him in his preparations and he had missed her presence and her bright chattering this morning. And then after he had been lecturing for only a few minutes it became obvious, even to him, that there was something wrong. He stopped and looked at the students with a puzzled frown on his face.

'Has something happened?'

The girls waited for Lucy to speak but she had welled up again and Alice, as usual taking on the role of spokesperson, explained what had happened.

Dr Ring hesitated for a second because he was embarrassed that his role in the matter was going to become public and then said, 'There has obviously been a misunderstanding. It was I, without Lucy's knowledge, who made the approach to the examiners, because I felt that she had been harshly treated due to her personal circumstances at the time of the examinations. I think we can abandon this lecture now because no-one's mind is going to be on Materia Medica no matter how fascinating it is (Caroline whispered sotto voce 'He's actually made a joke.'). I will go straight away to Miss Clegg and explain what has happened.'

There was almost a cheer though it was not clear whether it was because of Dr Ring's explanation or because it was their last ever Materia Medica lecture. The girls filed out, for once smiling at Dr Ring. Caroline went so far as to give him a little peck on the cheek as she passed, much to his confusion. Lucy stayed behind to thank him from the bottom of her heart for what he had done for her.

Dr Ring spent quite a few moments with Lucy as she poured out her thanks to him. She made no attempt to hold back her tears and Dr Ring ached with a desire to reach out to her with a fatherly hug so as to comfort her. But no, that would be wrong. And so, he just stood with her and offered soothing words. He tried to say that what he had done he would have done for any of the girls but that would not have been true and both of them knew it. Lucy was not so restrained, simply because she had a warm and loving heart.

'Dear Dr Ring,' she said. 'To think that you did this for me and I never would have known it. I have missed my father so much since he died but, during the whole time that I have known you, you have been like a father to me and I love you for it. You dear, dear man.'

And she stood on her tip toes and kissed him on the cheek and then hurriedly left before she once more descended into tears.

Dr Ring sat down heavily on his chair. It is not possible to describe his emotions. After the early death of his mother he had been reared by aunts who were activated more by a sense of duty than by any great feelings of affection. And, of course, he had never married. (It seems harsh to use the words 'of course' but that was the reality of his life). It followed that he had never had a daughter. And now his withered heart was exposed to the totally unreserved love of this child, as he thought of her. He was completely overcome. He could feel the fetters of the restraint, which normally protected him, dissolving and as the tension oozed from him he realised that he too was on the point of tears. He hurriedly caught control of himself and took a few deep breaths to recover. Then he set off to see Miss Clegg.

When he left the lecture room he was filled with confidence that he would quickly be able to relieve Lucy of the accusation which had been made against her but by the time he had gone the short distance to Miss Clegg's office that confidence had evaporated and had been replaced with the apprehension with which he normally approached any face-to-face meeting with her. Nor was he put at his ease when, having been given permission to enter her study, he was left standing while she remained seated at her desk. He felt like a disobedient schoolboy before his headmaster, with all the inarticulacy that implied.

'I was wondering if I could have a word with you,' he began but got no further.

'Should you not,' Miss Clegg glanced at the clock on the wall. 'Should you not be giving your lecture at this time? Are you unwell?'

It can be imagined that this query and the tone in which it was put did not reflect any real concern for Dr Ring's welfare.

Dr Ring was completely wrong-footed by this attack (in a conversation with Miss Clegg, Dr Ring categorised nearly all of her comments as attacks). He had hoped to bring up the subject of Lucy's Certificate obliquely but now he was being asked to justify an unauthorised departure from the College's established programme. He accordingly hesitated, fiddled with his tie, and said some inconsequential words much to Miss Clegg's irritation which she made no attempt to conceal.

'Dr Ring, I am a busy woman. Please get on with what you wanted to see me about.'

Dr Ring summoned up all his resolve. 'It was about Miss Dalrymple. I found her very upset at the lecture this morning and I wanted to clear up a misunderstanding which seems to have arisen.'

At the mention of Lucy's name Miss Clegg's brow darkened, or more accurately, became even darker. Her headache was now becoming more intense, but she ignored it, to focus all her attention on Dr Ring. 'And what, pray, do you have to do with Miss Dalrymple?'

Dr Ring stammered, 'Nothing really, I suppose but - '

'In that case,' again she interrupted him. 'I suggest you confine your attention to the teaching of Materia Medica for which you are employed in this College and leave dealing with students to those who are entrusted to deal with them.'

Dr Ring screwed up his courage once more. 'At the lecture this morning the students were in such a state of unrest that it was impossible to continue'

'That is just a nonsense, Dr Ring. You are employed here to lecture and if you are so incompetent as to be unable to control a classroom of young girls you might want to consider a different outlet for your talents.'

Dr Ring was in turmoil. Despite self-doubts he knew he had abilities. How was it that this woman could reduce him to such an incoherent mess? Then the memory of Lucy standing on her tiptoes to kiss him flashed through his mind and he returned to the attack – yes, the attack he told himself.

'You must listen, Miss Clegg,' he began again.

Miss Clegg's eyes narrowed. She was not accustomed to being told she must do something by anyone, far less by someone like Dr Ring.

'Miss Dalrymple had nothing to do with obtaining her Certificate. It was I who approached the examiners and told them of the circumstances around the time of her sitting the papers she failed.'

Miss Clegg frowned, 'And what were these circumstances as you call them?'

'The illness and subsequent death of her father, to whom she was very close.' Dr Ring stammered in reply,

'And how did you come by this information?'

'Miss Dalrymple told me herself.'

Miss Clegg had heard enough. She had wondered how Lucy had been able to gain access to the examiners but now it all became clear. How devious! Lucy had realised that Dr Ring was her link to the examiners and had wormed her way into his confidence and induced him to make the approach for her. And like a booby he had fallen for it. When he was appointed, Miss Clegg had emphasised to that lecturing to women posed challenges different to those met when dealing with male students. She had stressed that, to avoid falling into the trap of giving female students more leeway, he had to maintain an even greater distance from the students. And now this. She should have foreseen that someone as weak as Dr Ring would have been like putty in the hands of a manipulative minx like Lucy Dalrymple. She glowered at Dr Ring, 'I think I have heard quite enough, Dr Ring. I suppose there is little point in you returning to your lecture, so I wish you Good Afternoon.'

Usually when he left Miss Clegg's company Dr Ring felt as if he had been dismissed, but this time he did feel a quiet glow of satisfaction. Despite her normal aggressive manner, he had stuck to his guns and he had sorted out the misunderstanding over Lucy. As he closed the study door Dr Boring had a wry smile to himself. It was the last day of the term and, in a normal environment, colleagues would exchange comments about the term that had finished and best wishes for the summer break. He could not imagine such an exchange with Miss Clegg. If one had access to the innermost depths of Dr Ring's mind there might have been found there a hidden hope that she might suffer some dire misfortune over the holiday break, but such a thought was stifled at birth.

Before he left the College, he sought out Lucy who was with the Burton sisters and told her what he had done and that everything should be all right.

19

The final Assembly of the term was due to be held that afternoon and, after the upheavals of the morning, the girls were full of excited discussions about what had happened. Lucy told them about Dr Ring's approach to Miss Clegg and they waited to see what her reaction would be.

'Good for old Boring,' said Caroline. 'I didn't think he had it in him.'

Alice shared her sister's sentiments, but she wished she had not expressed them in what seemed to her to be such a common way. Before she had a chance to reproach her sister, however, the door opened for the entrance of Miss Clegg followed by the faithful Mrs Black.

Miss Clegg's headache had become worse in the interim and was now excruciating, although so far, her vision was not affected. In any event, as she entered the room, she was determined to press ahead with what she saw as her duty.

Miss Clegg strode to the front of the room and then turned to face the girls who were seated before her. She did not give her normal pause but launched immediately into her words.

'I regret to say that this term, which started with such high hopes, has ended so badly. Miss Dalrymple, whose eventual admittance to this College was obtained only by my efforts, has rewarded these efforts by the worst sort of deceit.'

She could go no further at this stage because of the violent reaction to her remarks. Lucy turned chalk white and almost fell from her chair. Some of the other girls voiced their horror and Caroline even started from her seat.

'Sit down, Miss Burton' Miss Clegg said sternly. 'I repeat, the worst sort of deceit. I would remind you that, at our very first Assembly, I stressed that you must progress by your own unaided efforts because any deviation from that principle would mean that any final success would be tarnished and put down to the help given.

'I must admit fault in seeking to obtain Miss Dalrymple's original admission by circumventing the regulations, but she has now betrayed my trust by going behind my back and conniving her way to a Certificate to which she was not entitled. In doing so she has brought disgrace on herself and on the whole College.'

There was now uproar in the room. Lucy was shaking with tears. She sobbed out that she had never been accused of doing a deceitful thing in her life. This time it was Alice who was on her feet.

'Miss Clegg, I must protest. All of us know Lucy. None of us would believe that Lucy would act deceitfully. She is the kindest, most truthful girl. Have you not spoken to Dr Ring? He has told us all that it was he, not Lucy, who approached the examiners. And he told us that Lucy knew nothing about it.'

Miss Clegg almost snarled at her, 'This is not a debating society, Miss Burton. And even if it were, your lack of years and experience would mean your views would carry little weight. My decisions in running this College, which are made in the best interests of all the students, are not open to challenge, especially not by the clique of which you appear to have made yourself the spokesperson. Having spoken to Miss Dalrymple **and** Dr Ring, it is clear that Miss Dalrymple induced Dr Ring to make the approach to the examining body. In doing so she was as guilty as if she had made the approach herself. And yet she guilefully protests her innocence.

'I am not having it. The success of this College, and of you as students in it, depends on a rigid adherence to the modes of conduct I have laid down. If you feel you cannot share this vision, then I suggest you seek your further education elsewhere.'

Then, as there were more outbursts from the students, 'There will be no more discussion. The matter is closed.'

With that she swept from the room.

Even before the door had closed behind her there was uproar in the room. Alice was trying to comfort Lucy, but in truth she was inconsolable. For a time, there was just a confused babble as everyone tried to talk at the same time but as the noise slowly abated one quiet voice began to be heard. It was that of Margaret Campbell. While all the furore was going on she had taken no part. She felt herself in an ambiguous position because she was fond of Lucy but she also, by living in her house, knew more about Miss Clegg than the other girls and knew how much she was dedicated to making the College a success and how much she dreaded the disaster if it were to fail.

Possibly because of that; or possibly because she was a little older than the others; or possibly even because, when a quiet voice talks through a hubbub, it somehow silences the noisier ones, people stopped to listen to what she had to say.

'I know Miss Clegg probably better than any of you and I know how passionately she cares for the College. But I know Lucy as well and I know that the allegations made against her by Miss Clegg are completely outrageous and must be withdrawn. But feelings are high at present and the further pursuit of the matter today is bound to make matters worse. I hope that you, Lucy, know that not a single one of us thinks that you have done anything wrong. Not one of us will countenance any suggestion of deceit by you. But it is a question of finding the course which has most chance of righting this terrible affair. The experience I have derived from my reading is that the more you drive someone like Miss Clegg into a corner the more she will fight that corner. I suggest accordingly that we draw up a letter in the form of a petition to Miss Clegg which will be from all of us, but which Alice can sign on our behalf. If we leave that with Miss Clegg before we depart today she will have the opportunity of considering the matter at leisure and without pressure and have the chance to take back her comments.'

Caroline and some of the more vociferous girls were against Margaret's suggestion as they felt they wanted to have the matter settled before they broke up for the holidays; but wiser voices prevailed. The most persuasive voice, because she was most affected, was Lucy's and this was sufficient to sway those who had previously opposed Margaret's proposal.

The girls then turned to drafting the letter. As can be imagined, when you have twenty people all with a high regard for their own point of view and a high wish to express that point of view, the initial discussions were lengthy and confused but they eventually resolved into two camps, one, led by Caroline, advocating a strong line stressing the injury inflicted on Lucy and demanding an apology, and the other led by her sister, regretting that there had been an obvious breakdown in communication which had brought about a misunderstanding.

The critical difference, it became clear, was the 'Caroline' camp's demand that there had to be an apology. Margaret Campbell, unusually vehemently for her, insisted that there was no possibility of an apology as such being obtained and to look for one was merely adding fuel to the fire. Miss Clegg had to be given a form of words which gave her, without loss of face, a way out of the position she had put herself but, at the same time, was sufficient to satisfy Lucy.

At length Margaret's approach was agreed and the wording of the draft letter with many deletions and insertions was settled. The letter began with expressions of admiration and respect for Miss Clegg together with a statement of renewed commitment to the College and the cause of woman's medical education. It expressed regret that recent events had caused such distress to both Miss Clegg and Lucy and it hoped that Miss Clegg would now accept that Lucy had acted honourably throughout.

With the wording agreed the girls all drifted off home exchanging good wishes for the holidays, leaving Caroline to read out the amended draft for Alice to make the fair copy. When that was done, Alice signed it, as had been agreed, on behalf of the whole student body and put it in an envelope addressed to Miss Clegg. When she had done this she suddenly became aware that Mrs Black, who had not been at the College since first thing that morning, had come into the room and had obviously been watching them for some time although she had said nothing and neither girl had noticed, as they were engrossed in what they were doing.

No matter. They handed the letter to Mrs. Black to be passed to Miss Clegg and, saying that they would see her after the holidays, left to go home, still a little shaken by the events of the day but relieved that they had taken action which should resolve the matter.

When the girls arrived home, they related firstly to Anna, then to their mother and later to their father, after he returned from his business, all that had happened that day. At Anna's suggestion, however, they downplayed the actual events so as not to worry their mother nor to anger their father. Talk then turned more generally to how they would spend their holiday time although, like most students, the first reaction was just to feel relieved that they didn't have the daily commitment of going down to the College every day.

20

In the first few days the girls devoted their leisure to doing the normal everyday things which their studies had prevented them from doing. In particular, they tried either singly or together, to re-establish contact with their friends because, during term time, they lived in a kind of bubble with the other students, concentrated on what they were learning and totally cut off from the social activities which were the daily lot of their friends and, indeed, had been of them, before medicine had taken over.

They both quickly realised there was a problem. Whether it was because they had simply lost contact, or because there were family pressures on their friend,; or because their friends too shared their parents' prejudices, they could not tell. The reality was that, if they were not exactly ostracised, they were certainly less welcome. But Alice and Caroline shared their father's independent spirit. They had done what they thought was right and they had plenty of things to occupy them now that the term was over.

One drawback of the holiday period was that Roddy had gone back to his home village. Both girls had become used to seeing him on a regular basis and when he was suddenly gone there was a void in their lives of which they were both conscious. If Roddy had had a sister they could have arranged a holiday trip to see him but, with no sister available it would have been highly improper, at least Alice thought so, to journey up to the Highlands to visit.

When Roddy arrived back in Kindrum, his home village, he was warmly welcomed by his father and his aunt who were anxious to learn more details of his time at university than he had been able to give in his letters. His aunt in particular fussed over him to an obsessive degree, but he put up with her attentions in good part and tried to get used again to his home surroundings.

Kindrum was a small village, set off the high road, from which a roughly made track led downhill until it became cobbled at the start of some cottages. The road broadened into a kind of square, around which were situated the only major buildings of the village, the church and manse, the school and adjacent schoolhouse, and the village store. The road, with cottages on either side, then led on further downhill to the shore of the loch. Apart from this, there were no other roads but merely little lanes leading off the main street lined with small cottages of varying degrees of decrepitude.

Roddy, returning from the big city, had difficulty readjusting to these surroundings. As the schoolmaster's son, he had always been a little different from his contemporaries; there was a standard of conduct expected of him which he had unconsciously adopted. As a child, when his friends were stealing apples from the orchard, he would be there but always on the outskirts. When they were engaged in the strictly forbidden practice of setting fire to the grass, he would seem to be involved but in fact was dousing what they had lit. He had a strong sense of what was proper and saw a moral dimension where others saw none. His friends were aware of the difference but accepted it as children do. And, of course he was further distanced from them after primary school, by virtue of his access to an education which was not available to them. And he was very conscious of this. Even at an early age he had felt how unfair it was that his closest friend, Calum, who was, Roddy was sure, just as clever as he was, could never pursue his education further, simply because he was the son of a poor farm labourer; he tried to help by lending Calum the books which were completely absent from Calum's house

It was Calum, because of his brightness, who best recognised, and did not resent, that Roddy had no choice but to be different and it was Calum whom Roddy sought out once he had become acclimatised back home. But when he ran him to ground, Calum confessed, somewhat shamefacedly that he had been going with a girl who was a maid in the local big estate and had made her pregnant; he was going to get married in a few weeks' time and he was getting by, doing seasonal labouring on the estate. Although they chatted on, both were aware that now they had even less in common than before and, after they parted, Roddy, who had so much looked forward to renewing their friendship, realised that they would never again share the happy companionship of their boyhood.

Others of his contemporaries were away working; some had emigrated; some, not surprisingly given the poverty of their circumstances and despite their youth, had died. On morning shortly after his return, Roddy was walking through the village somewhat disconsolately brooding on this, when he met a very attractive slim young girl who nodded to him as she passed, as if she knew him. Roddy hesitated, the turned.

'Janet?' he said.

The girl too turned. 'Yes, Roddy. It's Janet.'

Roddy did not know what to say, so he just grinned. Janet was the daughter of the local storekeeper and was about four or five years younger than Roddy. She had also been a tomboy who insisted in trying to join in the boys' games even though they were much older and, of course, much bigger. Roddy was fond of her because she just would not accept their rebuffs and he tried to protect her from their rougher treatment. In fact, he remembered one long hot summer when he seemed to spend most of his time wheeling her around in a wheelbarrow.

When he went up to university he kept his little friend in mind and, in his early letters home to his father and aunt, he always included a titbit of city life to be passed on to her. Latterly, as he now remembered to his shame, she had passed out of his thoughts and out of his letters, but he did not know that his aunt, for whom Janet was a special favourite, had made good the omission by inventing some gossip to be passed to Janet.

But the Janet who was in his thoughts when he was writing was Janet the tomboy, not this elegant self-assured young lady who stood smiling before him. He could have talked to Janet the tomboy without difficulty but, when confronted with this new feminine creature, he found his usual difficulty in speaking sensibly. She didn't seem to mind and, as he gradually gained some composure, he was able to have a pleasant chat with her.

As he went off home he could not stop laughing at the change in his young friend and he was still laughing as he told his aunt all about it, although she, of course, already knew. Thereafter, the high spots of his holiday were when, by chance, he met and chatted with Janet - at least he thought their meetings took place by chance.

As the days of his holiday went on though, Roddy felt more rather than less disconnected. Who was he? What was his place? Why did thoughts of little Janet intrude into his mind?

And, if asked, his friends and those who knew him would have had differing ideas as to the real Roddy.

Calum:

'I know Roddy John well. We grew up together. He's still nice and friendly but we have nothing in common.'

Janet:

'I know Roddy John well. He always took care of me when I was little. Other boys are after me, but I always hoped that someday… But now he has been to university he doesn't even seem to know that I exist. Miss MacDonald tells me about the girls he meets there who are studying to become doctors. It's no wonder I am not important.'

Mr MacDonald, Roddy's father:

'I know Roderick John well. He is a fine boy and my sister and I are very proud of what he has done.'

Dai Roberts, University rugby captain:

'I know Roddy well. He's a great man to have on the team but what a boy he is in drink. He's great at the singing after the games and knows all the words.'

A Vennel habituée:

'I know Roddy well. When he comes down to the Vennel on a Saturday night he's my favourite. He's so powerful but he's not rough like some of the men.'

Mrs Burton:

'I don't know Mr MacDonald very well, but he seems to be a very quiet, polite young man.'

John Common:

'I know MacDonald well. He is a sanctimonious country bumpkin.

House Surgeon at the Colonial:

'I know Roddy MacDonald well. He is the best student I have ever had working under me at the Infirmary.'

A patient at the Colonial:

'I know Dr MacDonald well. He is so gentle and understanding when treating me.'

Caroline:

'I know Roddy well. He is so clumsy, but he is like a big brother to me. Or maybe a bit more. Maybe.'

Roddy wasn't sure that he knew himself well, but one thing was for sure. He now felt himself to be a visitor to his own village where he felt himself to be under constant scrutiny; it was only in the town that he felt at home.

21

Before he had left to go home for the holidays, Roddy explained to Alice and Caroline that he might have to come up to the town from time to time for reasons connected with his studies. And it was extraordinary that, as it turned out, Roddy was so assiduous in his studies that he had to come up to the city almost on a weekly basis. So much so that the girls ended up seeing possibly more of him during the holiday period than they had during term time.

He developed the habit of calling on them in the afternoon. If it was a fine day they often went for a walk in the beautifully laid out and stocked, nearby park. From the very first Roddy became aware that Mrs Burton was keen to join in these excursions and, with his natural courtesy, insisted that she should accompany them, which, after an appropriate show of reluctance, she did. The walking was relaxed, and the conversations were easy as between friends. As is natural in such a group the walkers would move from one person to another and Roddy would give his arm in turn to each of the sisters and their mother.

Mrs Burton had a strong interest in flowers and she loved walking with Roddy and picking up hints from what seemed to be his almost encyclopaedic knowledge of them. At the same time, she, who had long ago given up trying to plan anything for a Caroline wedding, began to dream again. Of course, Roddy was provincial. Mrs Burton's conception of Highland living depended a lot on Sir Walter Scott and she envisaged Roddy in his home environment probably wearing a kilt and going to collect the cattle with his claymore in his belt. But she was sure that he was a diamond and one worth polishing until he was fit for the drawing room. And so, she let her imagination roam on. She did not, of course, share any of these thoughts with Roddy. If he had had any idea of Mrs Burton's picture of his home life, he would have roared with laughter as he thought of his father ensconced in the book-lined study which he rarely left.

When Roddy walked with Alice, very often they would exchange only a few words but that was because they were totally at peace with one another and talking was not necessary. In contrast, a walk with Caroline was full of non-stop chatter (on Caroline's part) punctuated with outbursts of laughter and constant changes of subject. Roddy was happy to listen and be entertained. He thought she was the most enchanting creature he had ever met. When Caroline was telling a story, she had the habit, which he found endearing, of pressing against him when she wanted to emphasise a point. And, he wasn't sure, but when Caroline took his arm wasn't there just a little bit of extra squeezing? (In this he was right. Caroline did enjoy the feel of that muscular arm linked in hers and she occasionally allowed her thoughts to dwell on that strong arm carrying her away from the riot).

If the weather was poor, or if Roddy was unable to call until later, he would be received in the drawing room, in which he was slowly beginning to feel more relaxed. Both the girls were accomplished pianists and they would play either singly or in duet for his entertainment. He declined their request for him to play the piano and explained that the piano teacher, who had been employed to teach the young Roddy, had come to his father after two lessons to return his fee as he did not want to take money under false pretences.

Sometimes Lucy, who had a lovely voice, would join them and they would give a little concert. A favourite was Gilbert and Sullivan and they would sing extracts from the operas with much bravura especially on the part of Caroline who twisted her face comically much to Roddy's delight and her mother's disgust.

Although Roddy was occasionally asked to sing, he always declined. He had, in fact, a strong singing voice but it had always been put to use in exclusively male company (and with an exclusively male repertoire) and he did not think he could adapt it to drawing room mode.

He was fortunate, now that he had been accepted by the girls, that it was not the season for balls. At home, he rather prided himself on his expertise on the floor, but it was in the kind of dancing more akin to Mrs Burton's concept of the Highlands, involving a greater expenditure of energy (and indeed perspiration) than was customary in the more effete city soirees.

Once, when they were sitting in the drawing room, the subject of their future plans came up. The girls already knew Roddy's ideas in connection with plants, but he explained at greater length to Mrs Burton how medicine was developing. He could see the attraction of surgery, but that was correcting something that had already gone wrong and until quite recently that was the main object of medicine. He saw the future in preventing things from going wrong and, where that was not possible, in treating patients in a way less radical than surgery. From his knowledge of plants and his studies in Materia Medica he visualised a future where drugs could be obtained from plants, as opium was at present, but to a hugely greater extent and this would transform medical practice.

Mrs Burton was no fool, but she had only a vague idea of what Roddy was speaking about. What she did appreciate was the intense enthusiasm with which he spoke.

'What about you, Alice?'

'When I have the qualifications, my plan is to put up my plate somewhere in a part of town where poorer people might not be afraid to come. At the very beginning Papa said that he would give his consent to medical training but that I should not accept payment for any treatment I should give. He thought that it was beneath the dignity of a lady to accept payment in that way. I did not entirely agree with him but that was the basis of his consent and I will abide by his wishes. And of course, it is most generous of Papa to continue to support me.'

'I entirely agree with your father's sentiments. It would be most improper to seek payment. But if you are going to work in a poorer part of town does that not mean that you may have to deal with the lowest classes?' Mrs Burton was shocked by the disclosure. She had from the first been against the girls embarking on what she saw as a calamitous course, but had eventually reconciled herself to the idea, envisaging that any actual work the girls became involved in would be, for example, sitting at the bedside of an aged dowager and mopping her brow while distracting her with some idle gossip. But this!

Mrs Burton said tentatively, 'But you will be dealing with people who will be filthy and who will have diseases. You will bring all that back to the house here.'

'Oh, Mother. That they may have diseases is the whole point of my being there. And the little experience I have had with poorer people is that they expect less and are the most grateful for anything that is done for them.'

With a sigh, but without much expectation, Mrs Burton turned to her younger daughter. 'And what about you, Caroline?'

'I'm going to become a medical missionary.'

This brought a gasp from Alice because it was news even to her. Roddy sat bolt upright on his chair. Mrs Burton reeled as she sat; if she had been standing she would have fallen. She started to speak but she had no real control of her tongue and the words came out totally garbled. Luckily Alice took over. 'Where did this come from? You've never mentioned this to me before.'

Caroline smiled. 'I'm sorry, Alice, but I have only recently decided to do this. Do you remember a couple of months ago, there was a visiting minister in the kirk and he was home on holiday from West Africa where the church had a mission station? He spoke of the terrible need of the people and it was his words that made me come to my decision. I am going to go where I am needed the most.'

Alice looked at her sister thoughtfully. This was a new Caroline and she didn't know how to take her. It didn't sound like it was one of the things Caroline might say merely to shock. Roddy didn't know what to think. Like most young men, he lived in the present and he was content with the joy of having Caroline in his company without thinking at all about the next step if indeed there was to be one.

Strangely enough, of the three, it was Mrs Burton who, now having digested Caroline's news, was the most relaxed. She said to herself, 'This is just one more of Caroline's madcap ideas. By next week she will have forgotten all about it.'

And having recovered she was able to turn the conversation onto more general matters until it was time for Roddy to leave.

Roddy, as he walked down the road, thought about what Caroline had said but then put it to the back of his mind. He loved being with her - or more accurately being in her company, because he had never been alone with her. He had often fantasised about it, but he had no idea how to bring it about or what he would do if he was alone with her. The extent of his erotic longings was to have the right to have his arm around that slim waist; he did not in any way associate his time with her with the drunken sexual fumblings in which he was occasionally involved on his Saturday nights. And she never once featured in his nocturnal erotic dreams although, incredibly, on one occasion, Miss Clegg did. It would have seemed to him totally improper to think of her in that way. For now, although he adored her, it was sufficient for him to feel that she in return trusted him and, he was sure, regarded him as a close friend, possibly even her closest friend. For him this long summer had been an idyll which he never wanted to end.

22

On the day of the storm over Lucy, Mrs Black had taken the letter which the sisters had left with her to deliver it to Miss Clegg, but most unusually Miss Clegg had left the College early and had gone home without any explanation. In fact, she was suffering from the worst headache with accompanying nausea she had ever experienced. When Margaret Campbell came home, sometime later, she was told that Miss Clegg had gone straight to her room with express instructions that she was not to be disturbed. The maid told Margaret that Miss Clegg had been as white as a sheet and had declined the offer of any food. Margaret debated with herself whether she should check to see that she was all right, but she decided that she had better abide by her instructions. Miss Clegg did not appear for the evening meal nor for evening prayers, which was unprecedented in the period that Margaret had lived with her. Margaret herself led the prayers and included in them a wish for Miss Clegg's speedy recovery. She expressed it to herself, as she was pretty sure that Miss Clegg would not approve of seeking divine intervention for her benefit.

The next morning Miss Clegg was up at her usual early hour and, in response to Margaret's query, pronounced herself fully recovered from the previous day's indisposition although to Margaret's eye she still appeared very pale. Because the holidays had started Margaret did not go to the College, but Miss Clegg set off as normal and arrived at the College where only Mrs Black was present.

Mrs Black handed over the letter entrusted to her explaining that she had come across the Burton sisters writing it. Miss Clegg realised, of course, that it would be about Lucy Dalrymple and, before she had actually opened it, her temper was already rising at the continued impertinence of those girls in questioning her running of the College. She dismissed as insincere flattery the letter's initial expressions of respect and ignored the declaration that it had been written on behalf of the whole student body. She knew quite well who was behind it. She jumped straight down to the end and the assertion, monstrous in her eyes, that Lucy was innocent of the deceit which Miss Clegg knew she had committed.

Most unusually for her, in her rage she allowed herself to lose her normal composure and with it, the ability on which she prided herself, to think clearly in times of crisis. She strode up and down her office unconsciously twisting and tearing the letter in her hands almost as if she was physically attacking one of the sisters. Eventually she threw the mangled remains of the letter into the wastepaper basket and called for Mrs Black. She appeared immediately, as the door to Miss Clegg's office had been deliberately left ajar by Mrs Black herself, who she had been surreptitiously watching through the gap.

'Contact all the Trustees and summon then to an emergency board meeting to be held either tomorrow or the next day at the latest.'

'Those Burton sisters again', said Mrs Black.

Miss Clegg did not answer but the look on her face was sufficient confirmation. As it happened, because the holiday period had already started, it proved impossible to gather even a quorum of the Trustees as quickly as Miss Clegg wanted and it was nearly three weeks before the meeting took place. In the meantime, Miss Clegg's anger had not abated, if anything, it increased because of the frustration that she could not progress what she had already decided should happen. The delay did allow her to recover her composure and she was able to plan her actions in her usual controlled way.

The Trustees had all been hand-picked by Miss Clegg and were all men   This seems remarkable, but it was a deliberate decision by Miss Clegg who was prepared to make this short-term concession in order to achieve her long-term aim and who had felt that only by doing this would the venture achieve the necessary standing in the community. In any event, from the beginning, she had regarded the Trustees as a regrettable necessity, leaving her free to do as she wished.

The Trustees gathered in what was ambitiously named the Boardroom but was normally used by the students for their leisure time. As they waited the arrival of Miss Clegg, they discussed amongst themselves the reason for this emergency meeting but even the Chairman, the local minister, Mr Bryden, was unable to enlighten them, as he himself had not been told.

As was her usual way, when Miss Clegg came in she dispensed with the normal formalities of welcoming the Trustees and thanking them for their attendance.

'I have asked for this meeting because events have taken place in the College which threaten its very existence.'

As she had planned, this statement had the effect of immediately attracting their full attention. None of them took much, if any, part in the functioning of the College but they were all known to be involved in it and would not want to be associated with its failure.

'You may recall the enormous difficulties which were faced in obtaining the hospital access for our students, which is crucial to the operation of the College. You will also remember that I reported to you some months ago, that because of the thoughtless actions of some of the students, there was a real danger that the privilege of access to the Colonial Infirmary would be withdrawn. It was only after considerable toing and froing that we were able to re-establish the status quo. However, the students who were principally involved in that matter continued thereafter to prove an obstacle to the smooth running of the College by their challenging of the rules which are necessary for that purpose.

'Now an even more serious breach has taken place. I had occasion to reprimand one of the students, a girl called Lucy Dalrymple, who was caught out in a deception involving last year's Education Certificate. She was the girl who failed two of her papers but was allowed, through my good offices, to proceed with her course provided she passed the requisite papers at this year's session. Recently, by chance, I discovered that she had gone behind my back and, with the connivance I am sorry to say, of one of the lecturers, approached the examining body with some trumped up story of ill health at the time of the examination and prevailed upon them to re-assess her papers and issue her a full Certificate.'

Although some of the Trustees were not fully aware of the procedures Miss Clegg was describing, they knew from her tone that the matter had to be treated as serious.

Miss Clegg continued, 'Having been caught out in this deception, this girl persisted in affirming her innocence despite being challenged before the entire class. This led to a violent confrontation involving the whole class, in which the two Burton sisters were prominent. These are the same girls who were involved in the Colonial Infirmary incident and in many acts of insubordination before and after. And then later my Secretary Miss Black caught them framing a letter which was thereafter delivered to me and which denounced my treatment of Miss Dalrymple and demanded an apology.'

This narration of events caused consternation amongst the Trustees. The last thing most wanted was having to deal with anything that ruffled the smooth surface of their lives. One expressed sympathy (which was met with a blank stare) with what Miss Clegg had had to put up with. Others made various fairly vacuous comments which in Miss Clegg's view were as much good as clearing their throats. But what was to be done about it? Miss Clegg fully realised that the Trustees were waiting to be told but she let them talk a little before she intervened.

'This can only be dealt with in one way', she said. 'I cannot and will not manage this College in the face of such insubordination. I seek your authority to have those responsible, Miss Alice Burton and Miss Caroline Burton, excluded from the College.'

This came as a shock to the Trustees. Quite apart from anything else, it seemed that, rather than carrying out what they perceived as their normal role of approving something already determined, they were being asked actually to make a decision on something which seemed major in the running of the College. There was accordingly some considerable discussion amongst them until they naturally turned to the Chairman for guidance.

'Is the proposed exclusion not a little drastic', queried the Chairman. 'I remember that the previous trouble was met with by a period of suspension and that seemed to work quite well.'

'That is not a remedy which meets the gravity of the situation,' replied Miss Clegg.

One of the other Trustees, who was an accountant and who was one whom Miss Clegg classed as a troublemaker, referred back to the difficulty they had experienced in attracting sufficient students to get the College up and running. He wondered how they would fill the gap in financial terms if these two were to go.

'That is not a difficulty', Miss Clegg told him. 'Once we were open and with the success we have had, we have had numerous enquiries from those who want to enrol. In fact, I had anticipated coming back to the Trustees to discuss future expansion.'

This greatly allayed the concerns of those who had fretted about possible failure. In the case of failure, they would have described their role as purely honorary. But if the venture was a success they could congratulate themselves on providing the sound foundation on which that success was built and without which the success would not have been achieved.

'Miss Clegg', asked the Chairman. 'Is this extremely drastic step the only way to deal with this unpleasant situation?'

Miss Clegg decided that it was now time to play her decisive card. 'Mr Bryden, it may be drastic as you call it, but it is the only way.' She continued with a wintry smile. 'If you will forgive the medical metaphor, to cure the sickness you have to lance the boil. Let me speak plainly. The position is intolerable. She paused. Either they go, or I go.'

Although they had realised that matters were serious, without necessarily knowing why, the Trustees were shocked by this announcement. But, faced with this ultimatum, the Trustees had no alternative. One or two said one or two meaningless things simply because they always said something at meetings; but the meeting was drawn to a conclusion by the Chairman expressing the Trustees full support for Miss Clegg's endeavours and giving her full authority to issue the letters of termination.

On their way out, the accountant Trustee said to one of the others, 'What I don't understand is what difference it makes whether or not the girl Dalrymple did go back to the examiners.'

'Oh, I didn't quite follow the reasoning. Anyway, it's done now and it's one more thing we don't have to worry about. It's good to know that there are new candidates coming forward to swell the ranks.'

After the Trustees had departed, Mrs Black took great pleasure in drawing the letters of termination to Miss Clegg's dictation.

23

The morning after the Trustees meeting, Alice was first down for breakfast and went through the mail which had been delivered. She saw, amongst the other mail, two envelopes, one for her and one for Caroline, both obviously coming from the College. Presuming they related to arrangements for the new term she put them to one side until she had read her other letters. Still smiling at the news in the last letter she read, she ate some toast as she opened her envelope from the College. At first, because she was expecting something totally different, she did not properly take in what the letter contained. When she read it again she nearly choked on the food she was eating. She still did not comprehend it. How could her course be terminated? Was the College itself to be closed? No. The letter stated that the reason for termination was 'persistent insubordination contrary to the smooth running of the College'. What insubordination? At this stage, Alice's mind was in a whirl and she was incapable of clear thought. Caroline had just arrived for her breakfast and Alice suddenly realised that Caroline's letter might be on the same lines as her own.

Caroline came in with her usual early morning smile but as soon as she saw her sister she realised something was wrong. 'Are you all right, Alice? You're looking a bit peely-wally. Has something happened?'

Alice was unable to speak but merely motioned towards Caroline's envelope and watched her as she opened it. Caroline read halfway through her letter, looked up at her sister, and then read to the end. She looked up again, this time with a fearful look on her face. She knew, as her mother had often told her, that she could annoy people with her irreverence especially to those in authority, but surely nothing as bad as to justify this. Just as she had since she was little, she looked at her elder sister for support and, at her request, handed over her letter. As Alice had expected, it was in exactly the same terms as her own. In turn she handed Caroline her letter. When

Caroline read it she felt, a little shamefully, a slight feeling of relief. At least the two of them were in the same boat and could face this together.

It was then that Alice broke down in tears. It had just come home to her that this meant the end of her dream of becoming a doctor. Caroline was horrified. This was her big sister whom she idolised; Alice was the strong one on whom Caroline depended. It was Alice who tended to her grazed knees and who comforted her when their pet dog had died. Caroline had never seen her crying. Caroline, herself now in tears, rushed over to her and the two sisters hugged and kissed each other until slowly they recovered their composure.

What was to be done? Alice's mind grew a little clearer. 'We must keep it from Mother until Papa comes home. You know how, as she has become older, things worry her unduly. Once we have spoken to Papa he will know what is to be done and how we deal with Mother. In the meantime, we will try and act normally. I know she has engaged to be out most of the day so that is a help. Luckily Roddy has gone back home so that deals with that problem. I presume no-one else knows about these letters at this stage although they are bound to soon enough. We will just have to cope with that.'

Caroline was not so sure that Roddy's absence was such a good thing. She had become accustomed to look to him for guidance on various matters but admittedly nothing as personal as this. Caroline so far had not worried about the consequences to her medical hopes, but Alice's words brought home to her the prospect of public disgrace when people found out that they had been expelled from the College. She felt her heart sink when she thought of it.

'Is it just us? She asked Alice. Is it the same for the others like Lucy?

Alice could only shrug in reply.

It was a long day. Luckily Mrs Burton was fully involved with her own engagements and did not notice anything amiss. The girls were too preoccupied with their individual thoughts to discuss the matter further, except with Anna to whom they talked separately throughout the day, using her as a sounding board for their worries. In this way they managed to fill in the time somehow until their father's return from his office. Alice had full trust in her father and awaited his return with as much equanimity as was possible in the circumstances. Caroline, on the other hand, was a little fearful of his anger when he discovered what had happened although, unlike many previous occasions, she was not sure what she had done wrong. In any event, she would let Alice do the talking.

When Mr Burton came home, Alice as usual brought him his slippers but when he went to his study to deal with that morning's mail she and Caroline followed him in.

'Papa,' Alice said 'I am afraid we have some bad news. This is a letter I received this morning. Caroline has a similar one.'

The two girls sat down but Mr Burton, once he had read the letter, got up and strode up and down the room. When the girls had come in together and announced bad news he had imagined that it was to do with his wife and was relieved when it was not so. This letter was still a major shock, but Mr Burton had the ability, which Alice had inherited, to keep calm under pressure.

'What is this insubordination they talk about? Is this true?'

'No, not really.'

'What do you mean "Not really"?'

'There was that one time at the Colony, which we told you about, where we were both in the wrong, but we apologised and accepted our two weeks' suspension as a punishment. But nothing since then, although, like all the girls, we have objected to some of the silly rules which are imposed, as, for instance, making us register in the College like schoolchildren every morning and every evening even when our whole day's work is going to take place outwith the College.' Alice took a breath then went on 'What has provoked this, I am sure, is the stushie that took place on the last day of term over Lucy Dalrymple's Certificate of Education. You know Lucy. She is a lovely girl. You won't remember, but she failed two subjects in her Certificate and was allowed to start her course despite that, provided that she passed them in a re-sit this year. Well, just before the end of term she received a letter from the examiners with her full Certificate which was being issued on a re-appraisal of her papers. Naturally, everyone was delighted with this news, except Miss Clegg who accused Lucy of approaching the examiners behind her back and when Lucy denied this she accused her of lying. This was all done before the whole class, reducing Lucy to tears, and there was a general uproar.'

Alice paused again for a second, but Mr Burton who had been following her words intently, said nothing.

'It later transpired, Papa, that it was not Lucy who had made the approach but one of the lecturers who had approached them on her behalf. Miss Clegg was made aware of this but refused to withdraw her allegations against Lucy. Following on this all the girls, and I do mean all the girls, including Mary Campbell who actually lodges with Miss Clegg, had a meeting and, at Mary Campbell's suggestion, agreed the terms of a letter to Miss Clegg asking her to re-consider. Also, as agreed, I signed on behalf of the whole class and we had it delivered to Miss Clegg.'

Mr Burton, frowned and said incredulously 'And that is it?'

'That is it, Papa. That is as true an account as I can give. And Caroline will back me up.' After another pause. 'Papa, even if I had done worse than this, would it justify crushing the dream I have held in my heart for so long of becoming a doctor?'

It was only when Alice said this that it dawned on Caroline that her own dream had been crushed as well and she sat looking at her father with her face suddenly pale and with tears in her eyes.

Mr Burton stopped pacing up and down. 'There has obviously been a misunderstanding of which you girls have been the victims. There is the question of the damage to the reputation of the family which we will turn to in due course. The first thing is to have this decision reversed. I will present my card at the College tomorrow seeking an interview with Miss Clegg and hope that I can make her see sense.

'In the meantime, you girls can be sure, it is hardly necessary to say it, that you have my complete support. We Burtons don't bend in the wind. Now what are we going to say to your mother?'

The girls smothered their father in hugs and kisses, somewhat to his embarrassment, and then Alice went to fetch her mother. When Mrs Burton came, in the girls bade her sit down and then told her what had happened. They were surprised at her reaction. They had expected her to become upset and blame the whole affair on their foolish decision to attend the College. But no. This was an attack on her daughters; this was an attack on the family and the family was going to fight back tooth and nail. Both girls got up and kissed her. Mr Burton smiled to himself. This was the girl he had married all those years ago.

Normally, of an evening, the different members of the family would be dispersed around the house pursuing their individual activities but this evening they unconsciously gathered together in the drawing room talking quietly amongst themselves. Alice thought it was as if there had been a death and they were gathered together for comfort. And they did draw comfort from it and each went to bed in a comparatively relaxed frame of mind.

24

The next morning Mr Burton was up at his usual hour and into his office, from where he sent a messenger with a note addressed to Miss Clegg. It confirmed receipt of the girls' letters and requested a meeting to discuss the position. When Miss Clegg read the note her spontaneous reaction was irritation that the note had come from Mr Burton at all. When would women take responsibility for their own lives? Her second reaction was to pen a reply to Mr Burton saying any meeting was pointless as there was nothing to discuss. She sent it round in the hands of Mrs Black.

Mr Burton had not expected such a quick and negative response; it gave him some insight into the difficulties his daughters had been facing. He walked up and down his room for some time, trying to think of a way forward, as he was still anxious to avoid all out conflict which would bring the whole matter into the public domain. Eventually he decided to write to the Chairman of the Trustees of the College, Mr Bryden, whom he knew slightly, asking for details of any appeals procedure he should follow so as to have the case re-examined. Again, he had this letter delivered but he did anticipate some delay before he could expect a response.

Caroline, when she rose next morning, had lost the slight euphoria of the previous evening. Her father had emphasised that they should tell no-one what had happened, and she had only reluctantly accepted this because she had so wanted to confide in Roddy. But this morning she did not wish to speak to anyone about the problem or indeed to speak to anyone about anything. She wanted to run away and hide, to escape from the reality she was living in. She felt she would hardly be able to face even Alice whenever she came down. Fortunately, there was still some of the old Caroline in her and she suddenly decided that she would go for a walk before breakfast to see if that would clear her mind.

It was a beautiful morning. The birds were singing, and the flowers were sparkling in the sun following some overnight rain. As she walked along to the park the pressure on her eases slightly and she began to feel that she could almost scrutinise her own mind. She remembered something that Alice had once said to her. 'The accusations which hurt most are those which contain a germ of truth.' She could not deny that she had chafed against what she saw as the needless restrictions imposed at the College and, as her mother had often told her, she was not one who would hold her tongue when met with opposition. Yes, the accusation was true, but she felt she was mature enough to accept that she did rub some people up the wrong way but surely not sufficiently to create such resentment as this.

And then there was the shame if, as now seemed likely, the affair became public. But she and Alice had faced public opprobrium when it became known that they were going to study medicine and they could face criticism again if their expulsion was confirmed. As she came to the end of her walk Caroline's mind had cleared. Whatever she had done was venial even if exposed to the public gaze. The fault lay with Miss Clegg, the shameful way she had treated Lucy and her gross over-reaction to being challenged about it.

Caroline returned to the house with renewed spirits and was halfway through a hearty breakfast before Alice came down.

Alice had spent a restless night. She had full trust in her father and hoped he would be able to do something to have the exclusion decision reversed. There was just this doubt in her mind. What if he were not successful? Once Caroline had put the idea into her head, her whole recent life had been directed towards qualifying as a doctor. She remembered reading about the early pioneers and thinking how impossible it would be for her to follow in their footsteps. And then Miss Clegg had opened her college right on her own doorstep. To have the prize in her grasp and then have it dashed away would be unbearable. And to think that it was the same Miss Clegg, who had opened this unbelievable opportunity to her, who now, almost on a whim, wished to take it away. Alice tried to push it to the back of her mind; she did not share her thoughts with Caroline who seemed in good spirits this morning.

All the girls could do now was to wait their father's return in the evening. When he came in they could tell from his serious face that he did not have good news. He told them about Miss Clegg's abrupt rejection of his initial approach and of his subsequent letter to the Chairman of the Trustees. He was hopeful that, with his admittedly limited previous contacts with the Chairman, this would at least open the way to further negotiations. They would just have to be patient. 'And especially you, Caroline.' he said, with a smile, to his younger daughter.

'I will be so patient you'll think I'm in training to enter a convent', replied Caroline. 'There's only one thing. You wanted us to tell no-one, but Roddy is bound to turn up; he's almost one of the family. I think he would be very hurt if we did not tell him.'

Mr Burton raised his eyebrows at the description of Roddy as one of the family, but he agreed he should be told so long as he was pledged to secrecy.

Roddy did indeed call a few days later and was told the whole story. He was, of course, totally flabbergasted by what had happened. Naturally, sympathetic, he realised that the best way of showing sympathy was to try to take their minds off their troubles by filling in their time and by entertaining them with as many funny tales he could think of both from university and from his village life. As he told the girls, some of the male students got up to activities which were immoral (he spared them the details) or illegal and frequently both, with no adverse reaction from the authorities. One escapade, which had the girls in shocked laughter, involved the Principal's carriage which some students dismantled as it stood outside the building in which he was lecturing and carried up to the second floor where the lecture theatre was situated. There they re-erected it on the landing complete with the horse which, with some hay, they had managed to persuade to climb the stairs, to be put back in harness ready for the Principal to find as he left the lecture room.

The waiting was ended by a further letter from Miss Clegg. What took place was that when the Chairman received Mr Burton's letter he went to Miss Clegg with it to discuss what should be done.

'I'll deal with that, Mr Bryden', said Miss Clegg, taking the letter despite the Chairman's half-hearted protests, 'Leave it to me. There is nothing to be done. The matter is closed and will not be re-opened.'

The College for the Education and Promotion of Ladies in Medicine

24 May

George Burton, Esq.
The Elms
Fordhill

Sir,

Your letter addressed to the Chairman of the Trustees of the College has been passed to me for my attention. I can only repeat what I wrote in my previous letter to you. A decision has been made in this matter and I regard it as closed. Any further correspondence would be pointless and unwelcome.

> I am,
> Yours faithfully,
> Jennifer Clegg
> Dean

This letter was received at the family home and Mr Burton took it with him, unopened to his office. When he read it, he was possessed with real anger, not the reactive anger when someone gives offence, but the deep burning anger mixed with frustration when gross injustice is encountered. He had prepared himself for such a response but had hoped, at least for his daughters' sakes, for a better outcome. The first thing to do was to lessen the impact on the girls. Accordingly, when he arrived home, instead of showing them the letter, he announced that the next step had to be taken as Miss Clegg had not proved co-operative. He had arranged to see his lawyers the next day and thereafter a court action would be instituted against Miss Clegg which he had been assured would be successful. In fact, he had been assured, no, advised, that there should be a reasonable prospect of success; which was as positive a statement from a lawyer as Mr Burton, in long years of dealing with them, had ever received.

The next day the girls accompanied their father to the chambers of Maxwell Tilston & Morrison, which were situated in the old part of the town and up a creaking staircase on the first floor of a rather stern looking tenement building. As Caroline later told Roddy, Mr Morrison, who had survived both Mr Maxwell and Mr Tilston by some twenty years, was himself both creaking and stern looking but he welcomed them very graciously. His room was lined with books, none of which showed much sign of recent perusal or indeed recent dusting, and heaps of papers were piled on every available surface including the chairs for clients. These he cleared for them by moving the offending papers on to the floor. After they were seated he brought in and introduced them to his son, James Morrison who, the girls were relieved to find, was much younger, more of their own age and, in Caroline's opinion, quite good-looking - although that was something she did not share with Roddy.

Mr Morrison, senior had already heard the full facts of the case from Mr Burton but, at his request, the girls told their stories once again. When they had finished, he turned to Mr Burton. Although the proceedings would be in the name of the girls as pursuers it did not occur to him for one second to seek instructions from them. It would have gone against the habit of a lifetime for him to have done so.

'I have discussed the matter with James and he agrees with me that we should raise an action against the College Trustees seeking your daughters' reinstatement, Failing that, repayment of the fees paid in advance, together with a claim for damages to compensate them for the hurt and injury to their reputation. I will deal with the preparation of the necessary writ but James here, will make any court appearances which are necessary.

'It is always possible that when the writ is served the other side may choose to settle out of court - I would, in their shoes - but, from what I have gleaned about the formidable Miss Clegg, that is unlikely.'

A warrant from the court was be obtained that day and the writ served on the individual Trustees at their home addresses the following day.

'That will cause a ruction,' said James. 'They won't want this brought right into their own homes. I suspect they will all go running to their own individual solicitors in fear that they might incur personal liability. We shall see.'

As they left, the girls shared a slightly malicious satisfaction that those who had put them under such stress were now to suffer in the same way. They were also glad that James Morrison was going to handle matters in court. Caroline wondered out loud if Mr Morrison Senior ever made his way down the rickety stairs from his office and started one of her flights of fancy about his lifestyle, before her father reprimanded her fondly and said that Mr Morrison might look physically frail, but his mind was as clear as ever and they were in safe hands with him. Caroline kept her peace but, in her mind, although she had seen him standing, she held this picture of Mr Morrison Senior in a wheelchair being wrapped up in a rug at close of a day's business and wheeled into a darkened room overnight, before being brought out in the morning and helped to prepare for the new day complete with a breakfast of saps and a liberal dose of lubricating oil.

25

James was correct in forecasting ructions when the Court Summons was served on the Trustees, not only at the College premises but also personally at their individual private addresses. Quite apart from the Trustees themselves, various of their wives panicked at a Court Summons being delivered to their door. It was obvious from the envelope that it was a Court process which they had to sign for and at least two of the wives took it in, with anxious glances up and down the road to see whether any neighbours were watching. One other wife took the opportunity of telling her husband that she knew something of this sort would happen when she had warned him against getting involved with this Women's College nonsense. The Trustee in question did not, in fact, recall any such warning having been given but had the good sense not to argue the point. The collective outcome was that although it had taken some weeks for the previous emergency meeting to be organised, this time the Trustees all managed to make themselves available that very afternoon.

The atmosphere at the meeting was also a good deal more febrile than that at the previous one and it was a noisy gathering which greeted Miss Clegg when she arrived.

As soon as she came in, one highly nervous Trustee accosted her, 'When you inveigled me into becoming a Trustee you assured me that it was a purely honorary position for form's sake and now it appears that I am going to be dragged through the Courts merely because I supported your judgement in this highly regrettable matter. I have received no recompense for the time and work I have put in nor did I expect any but not for one moment did I expect to incur severe financial loss for my efforts.'

This Trustee's total involvement through the year in fact consisted of attendance at three hour-long meetings at which he had contributed nothing. But Miss Clegg thought it diplomatic not to highlight that.

Another Trustee wished to tender his resignation, but Miss Clegg pointed out that, while he was quite within his rights to do so, it had no bearing on the case. She had been quite clearly advised that no personal liability could accrue against Trustees as individuals but only as the legal face of the College and it was the College which would bear all liability.

Yet another started to suggest that perhaps the wisest course was just to settle the matter by allowing the Burton sisters to return to the College, but one look at Miss Clegg's face was enough to convince him that it would not be advisable to pursue that idea.

There were various other assorted grumblings from different Trustees about the adverse effect of publicity and even from one who worried that the affair would damage his chances of selection at a forthcoming election, but Miss Clegg gradually managed to allay their fears. She stressed that the raising of the Court Action was typical of the rebellious nature of those involved, the very rebellious nature she had had to endure throughout the year and which had led to their dismissal.

Her feelings were little short of contempt at the way these so-called or self-designated leaders of the city establishment were crumbling at the first sign of pressure. If she had been so weak in the past she would still be occupying some minor secretarial position. When Miss Clegg first realised that Court Action had been raised there was a momentary sinking in the pit of her stomach but that was very quickly replaced by relish at the anticipation of the battle which lay ahead. Not for one second did she anticipate failure. One strength of Miss Clegg was her unshakeable self-belief. It was also a drawback as this led her, once she had determined that she was right, to ignore any factors which emerged subsequent to her decision and which might have altered it. And sometimes the emphasis moved from fighting for a cause, to fighting to prove that she was right.

It was eventually agreed that Miss Clegg should instruct the College's solicitors to defend the action and Miss Clegg when conveying these instructions added the gloss 'with the utmost vigour'.

The fear of publicity which had worried both Mr Burton and the Trustees was fully justified. Court records were a ready source of copy for the newspapers and, as soon as intimation was made that the College intended to defend the action, news of the dispute appeared. The Daily Register, below a headline proclaiming 'College Catfight', gave the story as much invented detail as it thought it could get away with. It reminded its readers that, from the very beginning, it had forecast that this unnatural experiment of female medical education would end in disaster and it took no pleasure (or so it said) in being proved right. It trusted that the action would lead to an end to this attempt to interfere with the natural order of things.

The Caledonian, which prided itself in dealing only in facts, took a much more sober approach. It merely listed the case, with no editorial comment, in its column on Forthcoming Court Actions. But the readers of The Caledonian did not need any comment. They knew to make a daily perusal of the cases listed in the column to see if there was anything gossip-worthy coming up and for those in the know, which included much of the city's middle class, this was certainly gossip-worthy.

The publicity also had the effect that the other students contacted the sisters. It was true; only they had been dismissed.

The Burton family read The Caledonian and, without admitting to reading the Daily Register, knew what it said. They were prepared accordingly to be faced with criticism and derision... No. That is not strictly true. They just didn't know what the reaction would be. When the sisters originally made the decision to enrol in the College they suffered an initial coolness from their contemporaries which manifested itself not in outright criticism but in more subtle ways. Social calls were not returned; invitations to parties dried up; excuses were made in response to their own invitations. As Caroline said it was as if they had some foul disease which would be spread by contact

Although they had been initially upset by this treatment, the girls soon recovered, and the interest of their studies, coupled with the new friends they made at the College more than filled the gap in their social life. As such, they had to some extent lost contact with many of their former friends. They were pleasantly surprised, therefore, when, shortly after the case featured in the newspapers, two of these former close friends paid them a visit and, as is the way with old friends, the four quickly fell into the same relaxed chatter as they had always done. Shortly afterwards more visitors came. And invitations were issued just as in previous days.

Caroline could not understand what had happened but Alice thought she knew. In the first place, they had become 'famous'. Most of their friends had done nothing and would do nothing in their lives and to know the Burton sisters was now a feather in their cap, which they could display on other social occasions to those who did not know the girls and would be curious to know what they were like.

In the second place (and it was typical of Alice that she should be so methodical in her thoughts) the original antipathy came from the horror even disgust at what they had decided to do and which many thought put them beyond the pale of society. The present case was divorced from the reality of medical study; it was a fight by one of their own class (and therefore a sister) against a forbidding authority. Many of their female contemporaries had secretly chafed for much of their adult life against restrictions which hemmed them in and they relished the prospect of sharing, if only vicariously, in a fight against authority.

26

As the summer went on, the girls' attention became more and more focused on the Court Action. There were frequent meetings in the lawyers' offices to discuss developments and, deriving from this, contacts with other class members arranging for them to be interviewed or as James Morrison called it, precognosed (Caroline liked the sound of that word), to see whether they would be willing and, if so, suitable to give evidence on behalf of the girls. They were particularly keen to have Margaret Campbell appear for them because she was a strong figure who was not so obviously 'in their camp'. The difficulty was her close relationship with Miss Clegg, having spent the year living in her house. Margaret, although reluctant to speak against Miss Clegg, had a strong sense of duty and was prepared, if she had to, to say in court that, in the incident involving Lucy, Miss Clegg had been totally in the wrong. Before giving evidence, she determined to inform Miss Clegg of her intentions and if, as a result of that, Miss Clegg refused to allow her to continue as her tenant so be it - although what she would do for alternative accommodation for the next term she did not know.

A consequence of all this activity was that the girls saw less and less of Roddy. It would have been inappropriate for them to call at his lodgings and they were not sure of their movements from day to day, so that he often called to find them absent and to be greeted with a note explaining where they had gone. They were, however able to share one moment of stress with him when James Morrison reported that the Defenders, as part of their defence, had alleged that the operators of the College had an implied right to run it as they saw fit and that included the right of discipline and to exclude those who would not conform to that discipline. If this was upheld, then the whole action would drop. The matter would be heard by the Judge in what was called a debate, which Caroline thought was a very stately way of describing the proceedings, at which the girls would not be present as it merely consisted in legal arguments. The girls sensed that James was worried about this - or it may be that James rather exaggerated the risk involved so that his eventual success would seem all the more praiseworthy. And successful he was, as the judge decided that the right of expulsion had to be exercised proportionately and that was a question which only a Proof could decide. James basked in their praise and Roddy could not help but feel that he was on the periphery, murmuring only ineffectual words of encouragement rather than being involved in the red meat of the case.

The case was down for proof in early October but in the meantime Mr Burton had been busy. Mr Morrison Senior had confided in him that the weakest point of the case was the demand that the girls should be allowed back to continue their education at the College. This was absolutely crucial for the girls if their dreams of qualifying as doctors were going to be realised. But Mr Morrison thought that, even if they were successful over all, this demand would give the judge particular problems. Even if it were granted, it would be granted against the Trustees and not Miss Clegg and Mr Morrison foresaw that a tough adversary like Miss Clegg would merely circumvent the problem, by herself withdrawing from the College, leading to its inevitable collapse. It would be a hollow victory.

Mr Burton did not share the problem with his daughters. He had moved from horror at the thought of them studying medicine to a passionate acceptance of their dreams. He could not face their hearts being broken when, if they won, it would all turn out for nothing. He found it difficult to hear them cheerfully making plans for the new term when he knew there would most likely be no new term. Perhaps, Miss Clegg **would** accept whatever verdict was given by the Court, ***but,*** lying awake in the middle of the night, he knew that was unlikely. Only once before, when his infant son was dying, had Mr Burton lain awake all night. His various business decisions, and some had been major, had never caused him to lose a moment of sleep. But this gnawed at his mind without ceasing simply because he could think of no way out.

About two weeks before the day of the Proof, Mr Burton had to make a business trip to the neighbouring university town. When he had completed the business, he was tidying up his papers when his colleague, John Shaw, enquired how the Court case was progressing, as he had seen reports of it in the newspapers. Mr Burton, without going into details, said all was going well and was about to leave when Mr Shaw said

'You know my sister, Victoria. She's a good bit older than me. She somehow or other obtained a medical qualification and she is opening a medical college for women here. She has obtained all the necessary consents. I think our medical men are a lot less stick-in-the-mud than your lot. She is due to start in October'

Mr Burton looked at him. Then he sat down for fear of falling down. Mr Shaw looked at him a little anxiously and asked him whether he wanted a glass of water. Mr Burton looked at him again and then he sufficiently gathered his thoughts to be able to explain the dilemma they faced in the Court Case. Was there any possibility that his daughters could enrol in this college?

'I don't see why not' his friend replied. 'The more the merrier, I should have thought. I'll tell you what to do. You get your girls to make applications and I'll tell my sister to expect them. I'll put in a good word for them. I'll tell her that they are nothing like their father and luckily take their good looks and charm from their mother.'

Mr Burton had rarely returned from a business trip in such high spirits. At least, whatever the outcome of their case, the girls could carry on. There was the difficulty of them living away from home, but Mr Burton felt that might be more of a problem for his wife rather than his daughters - he rather suspected they might quite enjoy it. At least they had the option.

When he returned home, he was as usual warmly welcomed back. It is one of the advantages of living in a household of women that you tend to be the focus of all their love and attention. Alice, in particular, was relieved that he seemed in better spirits, as she had been conscious that lately he had been a little withdrawn. When they had eaten their evening meal, rather than as usual retiring to his study, he asked them all to join him in the drawing room. Alice had a premonition; something was wrong. She felt her heart sink as he began to speak.

'I wanted to speak to you about the Court case. Now, I don't want you to be worried, but I have been speaking recently to Mr Morrison and he has highlighted one aspect of it which presents a problem. It concerns obtaining a Court Order which would enable you to resume your studies at the College. Mr Morrison feels that, even if the Judge finds in your favour, which he assures me he will, he will find difficulty in making a decision compelling the College to re-admit you.'

At this point he had to break off as both girls reacted so violently, Alice with her hand across her mouth and Caroline jumping to her feet and almost shouting 'But that's the whole point of the case. The money side of it doesn't matter.'

Mr Burton hurried to re-assure them. 'Let me finish. I am doing this very badly, but it does get better. A further point made by Mr Morrison is that even if we are granted the Order which we seek, it will be granted against the College and not Miss Clegg and she can get round it by refusing to teach you even if that leads to the closing of the College.'

This provoked a further reaction from the girls with both speaking at once and, amongst other things, voicing their low opinions of the law in general and Mr Morrison in particular. Mr Burton allowed them to go on for a little before he again spoke.

'When I first heard about this problem from Mr Morrison - who, I assure you, is not so lacking in astuteness as you appear to think - I re-acted in exactly the same way as you have. You possibly didn't notice that I have been in low spirits since I received the news about a fortnight ago and continued to be so when I left on my trip.' Mr Burton was possibly stretching his narration but, if so, it was unconsciously, and his daughters' attention was totally caught. 'When I had finished my business with John Shaw he asked me about our Court case and I felt justified in telling him of our fears, as he is not just a business associate but a close friend.' He turned to Mrs Burton. ' You know his wife, Elizabeth, my dear, don't you? We spent some time with them when we lived there.

'Would you believe it? He then said his elder sister Victoria has a medical qualification and she is opening a college there for women medical students this very year. And, if you wished to apply, he felt sure that you would have every chance of being accepted right away.' Mr Burton gazed at his daughters with the slightly smug look of a conjuror having produced a rabbit from a top hat.

Mrs Burton was the first to respond but as her response was 'I don't understand' it didn't really count.

Alice and Caroline were speechless as they tried to rationalise this new development. It was Alice he spoke first and even then, a little falteringly.

'I find this all so confusing and I don't fully understand what is happening but tell me, Papa. Am I right in thinking that whether or not we win the case we are still guaranteed to be able to continue our studies either here or with Miss Shaw?'

'Yes, my dear. You are quite right.'

Alice smiled slowly but Caroline let out a loud shout of joy and rushed over to her father to give him a fierce hug. For both of them, the change from deep depression when they were first told of the problem with the case, to extreme elation when he revealed the solution was almost too much to bear and Caroline having resumed her seat gave a great sigh and then her shoulders shook as she dissolved into tears. Alice, who went to comfort her, was similarly affected.

Only Mrs Burton remained reasonably calm. She had not fully understood the difficulty with the case. For her, they either won the case or lost it; she could not understand winning and losing at the same time, which is what her husband seemed to be talking about. The one thing she had grasped was that there was a possibility of her daughters having to study in another town. Where would they live? How could they cope on their own, away from home? Who would look after them? Mr Burton and the girls combined to assure her that these were not insurmountable problems, but it was to take some weeks before she reconciled herself to the possibility.

27

Mr Morrison was delighted when Mr Burton told him of the outcome of his trip. His advice was, however, to keep it a secret for the time being. They should delay making a final decision on the plea for reinstatement depending on how they felt the case was developing in court. In the meantime, application on behalf of Alice and Caroline was made to the other College and was received favourably. In addition, because of Mr Burton's connection with Miss Shaw, she was happy to leave the application on a conditional basis and to keep the whole thing quiet until a final decision was made.

Preparations now started in earnest for the Proof. Although he did not intend to call all the students as witnesses, James Morrison wished to interview them all to satisfy himself of a consistent thread in the evidence they would give. Although he would have deplored the suggestion as unprofessional, there was an additional benefit for the young bachelor in that the interviews gave him the opportunity of meeting a host of young ladies, individually and face to face, impressing them with his command of matters legal. In turn, the young ladies rather enjoyed climbing the rickety stairs of the offices and being involved in something so different from their normal way of life. The time for being nervous would not come until they were actually being asked to give evidence in open court. Old Mr Morrison was not so delighted at having his office regularly invaded by groups of noisy young women, but his son insisted it was necessary

James stressed to the students that it would not do to try and paint Miss Clegg as all bad, no matter how strongly they might feel. He explained that, when they were in the witness box, his initial questioning would be designed to establish how much they had respected Miss Clegg when they first met her. From that basis, he would lead them on to show how, from this high point, their regard for her had diminished because of her treatment of them, to reach a nadir because of her treatment of Lucy.

He had to be more specific when it came to the Burton sisters because they were they main focal point of the action, being at the centre not only of the general accusations of insubordination but also of the two particular instances which had caused trouble; the dispute at the Colony and the outcry over Lucy. With Alice, there was no difficulty. She had previously admitted guilt in connection with the Colony affair and had apologised for it and, under James' questioning, would repeat this. James had already spoken to the Lady Superintendent who had assured him that as far as she was concerned that matter was in the past and she bore no residual resentment. Equally, he felt he did not need to guide Alice with regard to the Lucy affair. In speaking to him about it she was perfectly calm and lucid, and he was confident she would be the same when she was giving evidence in open court.

Caroline was a different matter. James enjoyed his interviews with Caroline so much so that he had perhaps more interviews with her than was strictly necessary. And she enjoyed her interviews with him more than was strictly necessary. But that did not blind him to the fact that Caroline was a live wire and he could foresee that under skilled cross-examination she might allow herself to be provoked into reacting with vigour to anything which doubted her veracity. She certainly was bound to exhibit, in her responses, the very insubordinate attitude of which she had been accused by Miss Clegg. His solution was simple: Caroline was told to stand up, speak up and shut up. Rather than resenting his approach, Caroline quite liked the firm way in which this young man acted towards her and was happy, for once, to do what she was told.

When James had finished seeing all the girls and, in addition, Dr Ring, he agreed with his father as to how the case should be dealt with in court. As a result of this, James made a preliminary approach to the judge, which the sisters did not fully understand. In the normal way of things, as the sisters were pursuers, it would be up to them to prove their case first and for the defence then to rebut it. But James persuaded the judge that, as it was common ground that there was a contract in existence, the onus fell on the Defenders to prove that they were entitled to break it. The sisters couldn't see what difference it made but, as James behaved as if he merited praise for what he had achieved, it would have been churlish to have withheld the congratulations he felt he deserved. Anyway, it seemed to make both Mr Morrison and James happy, so they presumed it must be a good thing.

In discussing the case neither Mr Morrison nor James had any illusions about the toughness of their adversary. Mr Morrison reminded James about the funeral of his cousin, Mary Jane Wallace.

'Do you remember, James? Jennifer Clegg was there. Mary Jane had worked with her for more than three years, but she did not show a hint of grief. She is as tough as teak. She did not speak one word of consolation to Mary Jane's mother and did not speak at all to any of the relatives. She gave the impression that she was there merely because she had to be. I'll wager she gave Mary Jane a hard time. Did I say, "tough as teak?" More like hard as granite. You will have to be on your toes to cope with her.'

28

The Burton girls were not the only ones absorbed in the preparation for the Proof. Immediately the Court Summons was served on the Trustees there was an urgent need to appoint a lawyer to look after their interests in Court. Miss Clegg was not a Trustee and, therefore, was not, in theory, a party to the Court Action but, as can be imagined, she regarded herself as central to the whole preparations. Even though she had no knowledge of the legal profession, there was certainly no way in which she was content to leave the choice of a lawyer in the hands of her feckless Trustees. However, Mr Bryden, the Chairman, showing unaccustomed spirit, insisted that he needed to have trust in their lawyer and as such he would make the appointment. Unfortunately, he chose his Session Clerk, Mr MacPherson, a man of impeccable conduct but of a mild disposition.

In truth, there was no lawyer in the whole United Kingdom who the Chairman could have chosen, who would have met Miss Clegg's exacting standards, but Mr MacPherson was exceptionally ill-suited. After a period of three weeks during which he was constantly subjected to Miss Clegg's withering questioning of his performance, he intimated to Mr Bryden that he felt he should withdraw from acting as he did not have the confidence of the client (although Miss Clegg was not in truth the client) and, without that, he could not function properly. He also confided to Mr Bryden privately that it was not since he was a child that he had felt so much like throttling someone.

His successor would have to be someone of stronger metal.

Miss Clegg's lack of knowledge of the legal profession meant she could have no input into the choice of Mr MacPherson's successor, apart from complaining about whoever was chose:, again Mr Bryden was left to deal with the appointment. This time, rather than relying on personal contacts he canvassed opinions from as many sources as possible before he determined on a William Annan, who seemed to have most to recommend him - the primary recommendation being that it was generally thought he would be best able to cope with 'that woman'. 'We shall see', thought Mr Bryden.

Predictably, when Miss Clegg met Mr Annan for the first time, she was not impressed. He was a tall cadaverous individual whose handshake reminded Miss Clegg of the hand of a cadaver she had once dissected. His expression of sympathy on her predicament lacked any feeling. Not that Miss Clegg wished for sympathy: she wanted justice. When Mr Annan interviewed her to take her statement he seemed very distant, not seeming to be laying the required emphasis on mattes that she regarded as critical. He also, in her view, did not treat her with the respect which she thought her standing merited. 'Just another man with an assumption of unmerited superiority', she said to herself.

The only other witnesses whom he would be leading in the Proof were Mrs Black and the Hospital Superintendent, Miss Murdoch. To Miss Clegg's annoyance, despite her requests, he insisted in seeing them without her being present.

Miss Clegg maintained her grave misgivings but perforce had to keep her own counsel until the day of the Proof

Meantime Alice and Caroline were heavily involved in their own preparations, meaning that they had less and less time with Roddy. In addition, there was something else on Caroline's mind which she did not share with him.

29

Caroline was glad to be distracted by the preparations for the court case. In the late spring, she had noticed that their maid Anna was becoming withdrawn, totally unlike her normal sparkling self. When this behaviour continued for some weeks Caroline determined to speak to her to try to find an explanation. For this purpose, she drew her aside to a quiet spot where they would not be interrupted.

'Anna,' she said, 'You have not been yourself recently. Is there something wrong?'

Anna was immediately on the defensive. 'Oh, I hope that you are not unhappy with my work, Miss.'

'Not at all, Anna. Your work here is just as good as it has always been. But you are normally such a cheerful soul to have around the house, I miss it when you appeared distracted. Is there something wrong? It is not for me to interfere but, if I can, I would like to help.'

At first Anna was reluctant to say anything but eventually with Caroline's gentle encouragement she broke down and, between sobs, told her what had been weighing on her.

'Since our parents died, I have lived with my sister who is much younger than me. She's only just ten. There's just the two of us in a single room but it is good enough for us and with the money I am paid here we have enough to live on. But recently her health has been bad, she has a cough and no appetite, and she is now finding it impossible to leave her bed. And so, I have to leave her alone every morning to come to work relying on a neighbour looking in every so often.'

'Have you had a doctor to look at her?' said Caroline.

Anna made a small grimace, which indicated without words that, with her wages, doctors were a luxury which could not be afforded. Caroline, with all the confidence of six months' medical education behind her, immediately offered to go round to see her, Anna resolutely refused no matter how hard Caroline pressed. It was Alice who took Caroline aside and made her realise that Anna, who arrived for work fresh as a daisy every morning, was ashamed to let Caroline see the squalor in which she had to live and from which she emerged as if her clothing had been freshly starched by her own maid.

Caroline's next suggestion was more practical. 'I will arrange for our doctor to call and, (when Anna tried to intervene), if you mention money I will send you down to the basement to do the bootboy's job.'

The doctor was initially reluctant to make a call to the area where Anna and her sister lived but the Burton family were good-paying patients and he finally allowed himself to be persuaded. As he gave his report in their drawing room, on his return, he his impression was of one still trying to wash off the grime he had encountered.

Anna and her sister apparently occupied a single room in a top floor flat in which the individual rooms were let out separately and in a building which, to cram in more tenants, had been cheaply erected in the backcourt of an existing tenement. There were obvious signs of water damage from a leaking roof. They had access to cold water from a common tap but of course no hot water. The only source of heating was a small fire which Anna used also for the small amount of cooking she could manage. Toilet facilities were shared with numerous others but, as the good doctor did not think his remit extended to examining them, he merely conjectured that, given the way other tenants looked after their property, they would be in a disgusting state especially as the tenement backcourt was covered in overflow from a blocked toilet somewhere. He was able to report, however that, in the midst of this squalor, the room occupied by Anna and her sister was remarkably neat and tidy.

Anna's sister's Sunday name was Constance, but she was always known as Tansy. The doctor reported that she was about ten but, no doubt due to chronic ill-health, seemed much younger. She had a bright cheerful nature despite everything, but she was suffering from the advanced stages of consumption and, given the foetid atmosphere in which she lay, could have only a few months to live.

'But' said Caroline, 'If Tansy were moved to more salubrious surroundings and had proper nursing care, could that lead to a recovery?'

'No, not a recovery. But it might extend her life and certainly make it more bearable.'

'Right' said Caroline. 'Thank you, Doctor. That has been most helpful.'

Caroline spoke to Alice, who agreed; the two sisters spoke to their father, who agreed; and all three spoke to Mrs Burton. She was initially totally opposed.

'What would people say? I knew this would happen when this silly idea of you girls becoming doctors was first raised. Will the next thing be that my friends will want us to look after their sick servants? We will have a queue outside the door. We could put a sign up: 'Burtons Infirmary'. Would you want me to act as a nurse as well?' What would people say?'

Alice recognised in her mother the same flights of fancy to which she was accustomed in her sister, and she quietly diverted her until she eventually agreed.

'But on one condition. No-one must know what is going on. It must be kept in the household. And that applies to you, Miss Chatterbox' she said to Caroline. Not a word to anyone especially your friend, Mr. MacDonald. He would think this was a good idea and would tell the whole world.'

The big problem now was getting Anna to agree. It was decided that Alice, of whom Anna was a little in awe, should do the talking. She and Caroline led a somewhat apprehensive Anna into the drawing room and, despite Anna's reluctance, made her sit down.

'Anna, we have had a family meeting and decided that we would like to help you about Tansy. There is a room downstairs here, which is lovely and sunny and looks out on to the back garden. We would like you to have the use of that room with Tansy.'

Anna tried to say something, but Alice waved her down.

'Now, don't interrupt. Let me finish. Firstly, it means that Tansy can enjoy a more comfortable existence in a nice healthy atmosphere. Secondly, it means that you don't have to leave Tansy alone when you go out to work. You can look in regularly throughout the day to check on her. Thirdly, the doctor will be happier keeping an eye on her here.'

'And, fourthly' broke in Caroline, 'we want you to do it.'

While they were speaking, Anna sat twisting her hands in her lap. She half rose a couple of times but when Caroline finished she sat quietly with her head down.

'I don't know what to say, Miss.'

'Say yes.' said Caroline. 'You'll be doing Tansy a favour; you will be doing yourself a favour. I don't know how you can cope. And you will be doing me a favour. Otherwise I won't have a peaceful moment without worrying about Tansy alone in her room.'

Anna, with her eyes full of tears, eventually let herself be persuaded.

'Right,' said Caroline. 'I'll get Papa to arrange for the room to be painted and when that's done, Anna, you of all people will know where in this huge house you can find curtains and beds and the other furniture you will need. I think we can have all this organised to have Tansy in residence by next Monday. We must all jump to it.'

And that is how it was done. The following Monday the Burton carriage was the object of much speculation when it stopped outside Anna's tenement. The driver was not foolish enough to leave it unattended but had brought with him an assistant in the considerable size of the gardener. Caroline, in her enthusiasm, had also wanted to come, but Alice dissuaded her by, again, pointing out that Anna would not want it, but would be too conscious of the favour being done to her to object. While the gardener climbed the stairs with Anna to fetch Tansy, the coachman busied himself in dealing with a crowd of urchins who appeared from nowhere. They were all barefoot and dressed in a variety of rags and too big hand-me-downs. They showed no evidence of recent washing but were intensely interested in this stylish carriage which had appeared before them. One of the more daring ones asked for a 'shot in your coach, Mister', and another wanted to know the name of the horse. The coachman ignored these and other requests and kept the gang at bay with deft flicks of his whip until Anna and the gardener re-appeared carrying Tansy who, as the gardener later told his colleagues, added very little to the weight of the blankets. They then drove off with a trail of ragamuffins behind, trying to hitch a ride on the back of the carriage.

Alice had been worried how Tansy would manage on the journey, but they got home safely, and Tansy and Anna were soon established in their new room which, although it was in the basement, was at ground level looking out on the garden, because the house was built on ground which sloped down from front to back.

The difficulty at first was that Tansy had too many visitors, because everyone, whether family or servants, wanted to drop in to see Tansy who, despite her infirmity, had a wide welcoming smile, almost a grin which lit up her whole face. Even Mr Burton came to see her although Tansy confessed to Caroline that she was a little afraid of him and laughed when Caroline told her that she was as well. But Anna was firm and was able to set up a routine, which included the gardener who took it on himself to keep Tansy's room fully supplied with fresh flowers for his 'Princess' as he called her. In addition, when the weather was warmer, Anna arranged for the gardener to carry Tansy outside to sit in a comfortable seat of the garden where she could watch him at his work, chattering away to him when he was in earshot (and often when he was not). He rarely knew what she was talking about, but her cheerfulness brightened up his day and he often fashioned a little coronet of flowers to place on his Princess's head.

Of them all, Caroline was the favourite visitor. She gave Tansy mock rows if she hadn't been eating, telling her she had a dress ready for her once she plumped up a bit She had her in fits of laughter with her version of what had happened to her that day which often involved a certain clumsy gentleman. And then one day she accused Tansy of being a sham because she had been told by one of the maids that she had seen Tansy in the front hall sliding down the banister. At first Tansy was shocked by this accusation and protested her innocence, but then she realised Caroline was joking, and she was reduced to giggles. After that, whenever Caroline returned for the day, she made up some story which involved Tansy getting up as soon as Caroline left the house and roaming around the town, where she was seen in some escapade. Tansy, of course, denied all this but her eyes widened in delight when she listened to the places in which Caroline's imagination placed her.

One day, Caroline entered her room in triumph. 'At last I have proof,' she said. 'You were seen in Jacksons' (the town's main department store). 'It was the person who served you who told me, when I happened to be in there later. And here's my proof. You left your parcel behind and here it is, addressed to Miss Constance Burton. '

Caroline produced the parcel and gave it to Tansy to open. She did so very carefully with wide open eyes. It contained some beautiful red silk ribbons. Tansy gazed at them in wonder and then flung her arms round Caroline's neck and thanked her through her sobs.

'Nothing to do with me', said Caroline. I am merely the message boy.'

But Tansy just hugged her more and let Caroline tie up her hair with the red ribbons arranged in bows. Sometime Caroline felt her own heart would burst with the trust and love which Tansy poured out on her so openly.

All during the summer, despite the care she was given, Tansy was weakening but Caroline kept up her hopes and her stories. She had Tansy being spotted roaming all over the town; out playing games with the (non-existent) boy next door called William; sailing on the loch; even travelling on a train, a picture of which Caroline had to show her in a book as Tansy had never seen one. Then one day, after she had cleared it with Anna, Caroline spoke of how Tansy had been seen in the High Street between a tall man like a soldier and a lady with long fair hair. Tansy's eyes widened as Caroline told the story and her grip in Caroline's hand tightened as if it was the lady's hand she was holding. After that, whenever Caroline told a story Tansy would always ask if the tall man and the lady were going to be in it. And thereafter they always were.

Caroline also made up another story involving Jacksons, the department store, only this time the tall man and the lady had helped to choose a lovely dress for Tansy which she should wear as soon as she was well enough to get out of bed. This dress was cream coloured and made of silk and Tansy stroked the material as it lay on the bed beside her, before it was hung up from where she could see it from the bed.

Tansy had good days, when it seemed that she was getting stronger and she and Caroline made plans for her to go for a walk to the park, but also bad days when her little body was racked with coughing. Then, gradually, almost without Caroline being aware of it, or possibly blinding herself to it, the good days became less frequent. Then the bad days became the only days, and Caroline felt her heart breaking as her little friend always managed to summon up a pitiful smile to greet her when she came to see her. Eventually towards the end of the summer and just as the preparations for the court case were coming to a climax, the day came which Caroline had been dreading.

When she had looked in, before leaving the house, Tansy hadn't the energy to put her arms round her neck when Caroline bent over to kiss her. Now, when Caroline returned, she was met by Alice who said nothing but merely shook her head. When she went into the room, Anna was sitting by the bed where Tansy lay, barely conscious. Caroline wasn't sure whether Tansy knew she was there, but she sat beside her and smoothed her brow. She spoke to her but there was no response. She sat a while in silence and then thought, perhaps if she told her one of her usual tales, she might understand. And so, holding Tansy's little hand she started. She told of Tansy walking into the Gardens and being met by the tall man and the lady and how Tansy had run towards them and the tall man had swept her off her feet and then they had set off round the Gardens with Tansy hand in hand between them. As she told the story Caroline suddenly felt Tansy's hand tighten in hers. A little smile came over her face. Then her eyes suddenly opened wide as if she was seeing something in the distance. They slowly closed again. Tansy gave a little sigh, her grip on Caroline's hand slackened and Caroline knew that Tansy's days of roaming were over.

That night was a black night for Caroline. Inwardly she shouted at her god. Why did you make Tansy? Just as a plaything? She thought of the saying that one's life is like a pebble dropped in water creating ripples which extend in every direction and which mirror the effect our life has on others. But Tansy's life was not like that. It was like a drop of water falling on wet sand. Not a mark. What good did it do? In her rage, she beat her bed with her fists. She even found herself letting out a loud howl like a wild beast as she sat with tears streaming down her face. She must have fallen asleep half sitting sideways on the bed because she suddenly found that it was beginning to get light, and she realised that she felt a little calmer. Caroline remembered the totally unrestrained love Tansy had shown her. She thought of how everyone in the house had taken Tansy to their hearts and the grief they had shown when they heard she had died. Even Mr Burton, that stern unyielding man, had shed a tear when he was told, because he had almost come to treat her as a third daughter.

Caroline still could not make sense of it, but she was reconciled sufficiently to busy herself with making arrangements for Tansy's funeral. Mr Burton had, some time previously, purchased a lair for the Burton family in the main cemetery and he readily agreed to Caroline's suggestion that Tansy should be buried there. Alice, however, realised that they were making arrangements for the funeral without even discussing them with Anna. When she spoke to her, Anna said that she was most grateful for Caroline's thoughtfulness, but, when pressed, she admitted that she would prefer if Tansy were buried in her own plot which could be used for Anna and for any family she might have. Mr Burton was again more than happy to agree, and he purchased a new lair in name of Anna close by the Burton family plot. In doing so the girls discovered for the first time that Anna's surname was 'Simpson'. Servants, no matter how close, didn't normally merit a surname.

The funeral was attended by the whole family and most of the house servants. Tansy's body was dressed in the cream dress which Caroline had bought for her and was placed in a little white coffin which was carried to the hearse, then to the church and finally to the graveyard by the gardener and the coachman, the two who had first brought her to the house and who had asked for that privilege. When the coffin was laid in the grave the gardener stepped forward, looked down on it, muttered under his breath 'Goodbye, Princess' and laid on top of it a coronet of flowers he had picked for her that day.

30

Because of her mother's prohibition Caroline did not tell Roddy about Tansy and he put down her obvious preoccupation to anxiety about the upcoming Proof, the much-awaited day for which finally arrived about ten days after Tansy's funeral. It was much awaited not only by the participants but also by a large section of the female middle class of the town for whom the case had been a source of great gossip for weeks.

The Courtroom in which the case was to be heard, was a large, wood-panelled room with a raised platform at one end occupied by a long ornate desk behind which was a high-backed chair (almost like a throne, Caroline thought) for the judge and smaller chairs for Court staff. Immediately in front there was an area, enclosed by a barrier, with seats and tables for the parties to the case and their lawyers. To one side there was another raised portion almost like a pulpit from which witnesses would give their evidence. The public areas were further back and also in the balconies which surrounded the Court on three sides.

The public areas were packed long before the case was due to call. The noise, which was considerable, increased as the Burton sisters entered with James Morrison and then there was much craning of necks to catch sight of the famous or infamous Miss Clegg as she came in accompanied by her lawyer.

There was still a fever of expectation until the Court Usher appeared and with a loud voice shouted, 'Court', at which the whole courtroom following the example of the lawyers – and with much rustling of silk from the public galleries – got to its feet. The judge, wearing a wig and his robes of office followed the Usher, bowed to everyone (the ladies were not sure whether they should bow back or curtsey) took his place, and the case was underway.

The first witness was Mrs Black, whose version of the various acts of insubordination was elicited from her by the questioning of Miss Clegg's lawyer, indeed was spilled out by Mrs Black almost without the prompting of the questions.

Then it was James Morrison's turn. His initial questions to Mrs Black were innocuous and she happily confirmed that she acted as secretary to Miss Clegg, filed her correspondence, kept the daily register and generally dealt with the day-to-day routine of the College. She confirmed that she prided herself on keeping a good grip on things and, as far as she knew, Miss Clegg was happy with her work.

'Was it part of your job', asked James 'to observe the behaviour of the young ladies and to report back to Miss Clegg on what was going on?'

Mrs Black stretched up, 'I was proud o' the College and wanted to play a full role in making it a success and, aye, part of that involved telling Miss Clegg what the young ladies were up to.' (It will be noted that under the stress of the occasion Mrs Black from time to time let her language fall back into the comfort zone of her earlier years).

'Some might say you were acting as a spy for Miss Clegg.'

'That's a nasty way of putting it. Ah kent how much Miss Clegg wanted the College to be a success. Ah was merely doin' ma bit.'

'You have described to my colleague all you know about what we can conveniently call the Hospital Incident and the Certificate Incident. Can you tell us about any other incidents?'

'There werenae any other major incidents as such. Just a general reluctance to bide by the rules. They would shrug their shoulders and look at each other whenever I passed on Miss Clegg's instructions.'

'Can you recall anything that was said?'

'No, but a woman can do a great deal by a look or a toss of the head or a whisper.'

'I see,' said James. 'Let us pass on to another aspect of alleged rule-breaking - time-keeping. You have stated that both the Misses Burton were frequently late in arriving for registration. To your knowledge were they ever late for a lecture?'

'Ah wouldn't know about that.'

'Yes, but if they were to say under oath that they had never been late for a lecture you would be unable to contradict them.'

'Ah suppose no', but ah'd be very surprised.'

'Let us turn to attendance,' said James. 'A most important aspect of College discipline. One of your duties was to keep a record of students' attendances, was it not? Can you tell the Court what was the attendance record of the two Burton sisters?'

'Ah couldnae say.'

'Or possibly do not choose to say. If I were to tell you that Miss Alice Burton had a perfect attendance record and that Miss Caroline Burton missed only one day, and that was the day after she was injured in the infamous Apothecaries Hall riot, would you not accept that that is an exemplary attendance record?'

Mrs Black knew exactly what the attendance record was, but she had not been prepared for this angle of attack. She couldn't think quickly enough how to minimise the importance of the attendance record when set against other examples of misconduct and so said nothing.

James pressed her for an answer, but, as she continued to hesitate, he said that the Court could take it from her silence that the attendance record was indeed exemplary

He then turned to the day of the Certificate Incident. Miss Black conceded that she had been absent most of the day and that the evidence she had given about it must have been based to a large extent on what she had learned from Miss Clegg. She confirmed that when she returned to the College all the students had gone apart from the Burton sisters, whom she found writing a letter that they subsequently asked her to deliver to Miss Clegg.

James pressed her,

'This letter which you saw them finishing, you naturally assumed was their own work and that was what you told Miss Clegg. You were not to know that they had merely been transcribing from a draft previously adjusted with the approval of all the students.'

'That letter was just typical of the way they behaved.'

'Ah, this letter. What did it say?'

'Ah don't know. Ah didnae read it.'

'But after Miss Clegg read it she would pass it to you for filing would she not?' Because she relied on you to keep her papers in order. She knew just how efficient you were. Did you file it?'

'She didnae pass the letter to me.'

'And so, this letter, which apparently triggered off the attempted exclusion of my clients from the College, of all the letters in Miss Clegg's files, has mysteriously disappeared.'

Mrs Black responded stoutly that she filed letters which Miss Clegg passed to her but there could well be others which Miss Clegg chose not to pass.

James posed one final question,

'Is it not the case that the students as a whole, possibly, were reluctant to take orders from you who had been put in a position of authority without having any qualifications; or indeed any aptitude for the role? And it was this disinclination towards you (James putting great emphasis on the 'you') which you then reported to Miss Clegg as insubordination towards her?'

'I dinna know what you mean by disclination. But students are aye an unruly lot.'

Much to her relief Mrs Black was then released from the witness box having survived the ordeal which she had been dreading.

The next witness was the Chairman of the Trustees. He explained to his own lawyer, Mr Annan, how Miss Clegg had reported matters and that the individual Trustees had no direct knowledge of the complaints made against the Burton sisters. Under cross-examination he confirmed that all the Trustees had been approached by Miss Clegg to sit on the Board and that there was an anomalous situation in that they were de facto appointed by Miss Clegg, but she then was their employee. His recollection of the Hospital Incident was that, at the time it was serious, but once dealt with, no further problems had arisen in that regard. The Certificate Incident was taken much more seriously by Miss Clegg. The Trustees had suggested a period of suspension might have dealt with the matter, but Miss Clegg was adamant. In her view the spirit of insurrection threatened the whole College. She said that personally she could not conduct the College with the Burton sisters in it. If they were not expelled the College must find another Dean.

After confirming that the rules of the College did not allow for any appeal in such matters, the Chairman was allowed to step down, to be followed into the witness box by the Lady Superintendent of the Colonial Hospital, Miss Murdoch. She confirmed that the Hospital Incident had, at the time, caused ill-feelings between herself and certain of the students. She explained,

'You must remember' she explained, 'that I was not used to having students in my Infirmary and the students were not, at first, able to adjust to the strict discipline necessary for the smooth running of a hospital. But I must stress that, when the matter had been dealt with by Miss Clegg, there were thereafter no difficulties and I had good relationships with them all.'

When James pressed her, in cross-examination, about her subsequent relations with the Burton sisters she replied,

'Miss Caroline was always a bundle of fun. We used to joke about what had happened.'

'And Miss Burton?'

'Once I came to know Miss Burton better I regarded her as an asset to the Infirmary.'

To Miss Clegg's ill-concealed fury, her lawyer allowed this last statement to go unchallenged in re-examination and failed to re-focus the witness' evidence on the Burtons' initial misbehaviour.

The next witness due was Miss Clegg. However, at the Judge's suggestion, as the examination of the witnesses who had already spoken had taken up most of the morning the proceedings were adjourned until the afternoon so that there would be a continuity in the evidence being given by Miss Clegg.

Over a light lunch, during the break, James discussed with the two sisters and Mr Burton how the morning session had gone. James confirmed their own feelings that all was going smoothly.

31

The Court re-assembled with Miss Clegg in the witness box. She was dressed in her usual black and was almost parchment pale which was understandable in the circumstances. She stood ramrod straight in, with her hands resting on the rail in front of her, and answered the preliminary questions put by Mr Annan, in a loud confident voice. Having elicited from her the difficulties she had overcome in getting the College off the ground he turned to the Hospital Incident. She confirmed that obtaining hospital visiting rights was an indispensable part of the viability of the College and without these rights, which were negotiated only after rejections from all other hospitals in the area, the College could not operate. The conduct of the sisters had put at risk the continuation of these rights and that was why she had taken such a strong stance in the matter. Quite apart from their conduct at the hospital, Miss Alice Burton had shown flagrant disobedience and deceit in sending the second letter to Miss Murdoch. In fact, she had been minded to expel them there and then, but had been persuaded to settle merely for suspension.

During the remainder of the term Miss Clegg had been aware both from her own observation and from reports by Mrs Black that the conduct of the two sisters continued to be utterly subversive of authority and in her opinion quite intolerable.

She was then led on to discuss the Certificate Incident.

'The only reason I found out that Miss Dalrymple had received her full certificate was that I asked her one morning how her preparations were progressing for her to re-sit the necessary papers. Only then did she admit to having already been granted the full certificate. I regarded that to have been devious in the extreme. If she had obtained the full certificate by honest means, I should have expected her to have come to me with the news. Her failure to do so showed quite clearly that she had obtained the full certificate by dishonest means and I told her so.'

'And you repeated your admonition in an open session with all the students?'

'Yes. I regarded it as necessary for the proper running of the College that the highest standards should be maintained – and should be seen to be maintained. I wished to make it clear that conduct like that of Miss Dalrymple had no place in the College.'

'And what transpired after you spoke?'

'I think Miss Dalrymple may have lapsed into tears. What I had said was true and people who have been pampered all their lives can't face the truth. And then some of the other students, including in particular the Burton sisters, tried to intervene on her behalf although what right they had to become involved in a matter concerning only Miss Dalrymple and myself I cannot imagine.'

'Afterwards, I believe Dr Ring came to see you.'

'Yes. The students carried on their insubordinate behaviour into their next class which was Materia Medica and prevailed on Dr Ring to speak to me on Miss Dalrymple's behalf. He stated that it was he rather than Miss Dalrymple who had made the direct approach to the examiners. That did not surprise me because I had noticed as the term went on that Miss Dalrymple was acting almost as Dr Ring's assistant and I found her spending a great deal of time in connection with preparations for the class of Materia Medica. But it did solve something which had puzzled me, which was how did Miss Dalrymple have access to the examiners. She had obviously wheedled her way into his confidence and achieved her objective through him. Men can be easily managed by a woman.'

The judge, who had not been easily managed by a woman since his nursery days, raised his eyebrows at this but said nothing.

'And you subsequently received a letter, is that right?'

'I did. As it was merely a further example of impudence I threw into the wastepaper bin as soon as I read it. Those behind it seemed to believe that the College was run as a sort of debating society in which each must have a say. That is not the case. One of the main purposes of the College, and it is one which I stressed on my first meeting with the students, is to foster the discipline which will be needed in future medical practice. An indispensable part of that discipline is to accept, without complaining, and I emphasise ***without complaining***, whatever rules and regulations one has to operate under.'

Whilst saying the foregoing, Miss Clegg's voice had become slightly more strident and she added emphasis with a pointed finger. She then answered some further routine questions before James Morrison rose to his feet to start his cross-examination.

There are few lawyers who can resist the theatricality of an open court session with an attentive audience and James Morrison standing in a court in which the public benches were filled to overflowing mostly with women, was only human. He bowed to the judge, looked at Miss Clegg, moved some papers on the desk in front of him, then put them back in position again, and eventually, like a consummate actor, when he was assured that very eye was on him, turned to Miss Clegg.

He started by congratulating Miss Clegg on her career to date and on her success in establishing the College. As can be imagined this praise had no effect on Miss Clegg, who merely looked grimly at him with compressed lips waiting for the counter thrust to come. He then went on to applaud not only the establishment of the College but its success once it began to operate. Again, Miss Clegg waited for the attack to begin.

'I understand that the young ladies at the College, in the course of the year, sat a number of examinations which were open also to the male medical students. Is that correct?'

'It is.'

'If the total number of students sitting was about one hundred and twenty, am I right in believing that the results of the lady students put all of them in the top half of that number?'

'I do not have the figures before me, but you may be right.'

'You must have been very proud. And am I right in saying further, that of all the lady students the two Burton sisters had the best results? At this statement Miss Clegg pursed her lips dismissively but said nothing. James continued, 'Is it not extraordinary that despite that success, you sought, for reasons which remain obscure, to exclude from your College the two students who on any reasonable criteria were its shining lights?'

Miss Clegg glared at him *'**All** the students came to me with high academic qualifications. **All** acquired medical knowledge in the course of the year. But you need more than that to become a doctor. You need discipline, not externally imposed but discipline from within. Self-discipline. You need to be able to meet difficulties without complaint. You need to take instructions which are contrary to your own opinions. You need character. That, not medical knowledge, it was my job to teach and it was in those attributes that they failed.'

James was nonplussed. He had planned to use the sisters' academic success as a weapon against Miss Clegg, but she had treated that as irrelevant and had turned the focus round so that the emphasis he was about to place on the sisters' attendance record now seemed of little importance. He searched through his notes while trying to rearrange his thoughts, realising that it would be obvious to all that he had been put on the back foot. For some reason, he thought of the discussion he had had with his father about Mary Jane Wallace's funeral. He turned to her again.

'Is it not the case that the standards you set yourself are impossible for ordinary mortals and that they can even lead to a tragedy? Like the preventable premature death of Mary Jane Wallace who was once your assistant and who died trying to live up to them?'

No-one in the courtroom knew who Mary Jane Wallace was but they saw how the mention of her name shook Miss Clegg. Her grip on the rail in front of her tightened, the little colour which had returned to her cheeks while giving evidence drained away, and she almost swayed on her feet. Within herself, she had always blamed herself for Mary Jane's death but to hear it publicly stated was a deeply felt blow. She tried to speak but words failed her. Luckily for her the Judge came to her rescue by stating, after checking his papers, that there was no mention of a Mary Jane Wallace in the written pleadings and that there was no Mary Jane Wallace in the list of students he had before him. When he was told by James that she was not in fact one of the students, he told him to abandon that line of examination and stick to relevant matters.

James said he was obliged to his Lordship, but he had recovered his composure and knew where he was heading now. Relying on information he had obtained from Mary Campbell, who lodged with Miss Clegg, he asked her how many staff she employed at present in total both in her private dwelling and at the College. She answered cautiously (because she wasn't sure the reason for the question) about twenty in total.

'How many of the staff you employ now, were employed by you at the opening of the College? If I were to suggest that, with the exception of Mrs Black, none of the original staff are with you now, would you agree?'

Miss Clegg replied coldly that she took little interest in the staffing of the establishments and she repeated this disclaimer when James put it to her that staff in a considerable number of positions had been replaced two or three times in the course of the year.

'Is it not the case that you set standards which only you can observe and that you reject as unworthy those who can't attain these impossible standards?'

Miss Clegg stated that she was happy to agree that she looked for high standards. But these were not just possible, but necessary, for those who wished to further themselves in medicine.

James then turned to Miss Clegg's own career. He obtained a grudging admission from her that becoming qualified as a doctor was the fulfilment of a long-held dream and that the founding of the College was her way of enabling other women to fulfil their dreams.

'Let us turn to Miss Alice Burton. We will hear from her in evidence that it is her long-held dream to qualify as a doctor so that she can bring medical assistance to those in the poorest parts of our community. I put it to you that, totally callously, you smashed that dream, by expelling her. Miss Caroline Burton will tell us in evidence that her dream was to become a medical missionary in Africa and I put it to you that her dream is in tatters because of your cruel treatment. I put it to you that, for all your fine achievements, your actions are the actions of a bully who revels in her power and who gives no thought to the consequences of her actions.'

During the foregoing James had become increasingly heated and Miss Clegg, in turn, responded in anger.

'I put it to you, young man that you are talking arrant nonsense.'

The judge at this stage intervened. 'Miss Clegg, I would ask you not to allow your feelings to run away from you when you are responding to questions. And, Mr Morrison, I would remind you that in cross-examination you are required to proceed by way of questions. Making a long statement with a rising inflexion at the end does not constitute a question.'

James bowed in acknowledgement then turned again to Miss Clegg.

'Can I turn to the Hospital Incident? The Pursuers admitted at the time that they were in the wrong, and they will repeat that admission when giving evidence later. Can you tell the Court why time-keeping was so important in this connection?'

'For the working of my College, my students required to have access to hospital facilities and the Colonial Hospital was the only one which would agree those facilities with me. Had those facilities been withdrawn it would have been fatal to the College.'

'And you no doubt explained all this to your students before they first visited the Hospital?'

'It is not my habit to justify to students the reasoning behind the regulations which I set down.'

'And so, the students were not to know that this particular rule was different from other trivial regulations like making it necessary for them to present themselves at the College premises at nine in the morning even though their lecture might not start till much later and might not even be taking place in the College premises?'

'The way I run my College is not open for discussion either by you or by any of the students who were enrolled.'

'I see. Let us now turn to the Certificate Incident. While the medical authorities made the possession of a Certificate of Education a prerequisite of medical training, the relevant examinations were run by any independent body unconnected to the study of medicine. I believe I am right in saying that? And so, the granting of the Certificate was a private matter between the education authorities and Miss Dalrymple. How on earth did you imagine that you had any right at all to interfere with the process?'

Miss Clegg was in a quandary. How could she explain her belief that the path to success for women in medicine could only be followed by denial of all outside assistance whether from men or from the use of what she scornfully regarded as female wiles. Such assistance was an admission of weakness which ultimately would bring disaster. 'Miss Dalrymple obtained her Certificate by underhand methods either on her own or with the help of Dr Ring. It was my job to train my students always to take the straight road no matter the cost. When there are two options the correct course is to have the discipline to choose the harder one. Miss Dalrymple was not bad; she was weak.'

'And yet you chose to upbraid Miss Dalrymple in public, to describe her as dishonest and devious and to speak to her in words which other students when giving evidence will describe as malevolent and vicious.'

'That is not true. Miss Dalrymple was a popular girl and that has coloured some peoples' recollections. I spoke strongly, yes, because I felt strongly that she had let down the whole College.'

James shook his head and before sitting down, to Miss Clegg's fury, said 'Is it not you who has let the College down?'

After further re-examination by her own lawyer Miss Clegg, was allowed to stand down and the judge adjourned the case until the next day.

32

After the conclusion of the day's proceedings the two girls and their father returned with James to his office to talk over with Mr Morrison what had happened in the Court. Although the girls were excited they were also very tired and Mr Morrison explained that this was the natural reaction to a day in Court, when one's whole attention is totally concentrated for such a long period. Even James confessed to being weary and he gladly accepted his father's offer to him and Mr Burton of a little stiffener; the girls settled for a pot of tea.

The girls praised James to his father and, while he was happy to bask in the praise, he merely conceded that the day had gone reasonably well. But he admitted that, in Miss Clegg, he had found a formidable adversary.

'Just when you think you have her at a disadvantage she suddenly changes direction and you find that you instead are on the defensive.'

'Don't we just know it,' said Alice. 'But who was that Mary Jane Wallace you asked her about? The mention of her name certainly had quite an effect on Miss Clegg.'

'Quite honestly, I had no intention of referring to her, but Miss Clegg had completely thrown me. I had agreed with my father that one of our strongest lines of argument was to emphasise your academic success, but she immediately nullified that by saying that academic success was almost irrelevant; it was character with a capital 'C' that mattered. I was merely trying to give myself time to think and I knew about Mary Jane because she was a distant relative of ours. I remembered that she had worked with Miss Clegg and had died in her early twenties, but I was taking a chance linking her death with the burden of work imposed on her by Miss Clegg. My father will tell you that I broke one of the basic rules of cross-examination by raising something to which I did not know the answer, but it certainly worked. It was the only time in the whole day that Miss Clegg lost her composure and it put me back to a position when I could attack her impossible standards.'

Caroline repeated how well James had done but Mr Morrison merely made a growling noise deep down in his throat and asked about the plan for the next day.

James stated that, although he would have some in reserve if the chosen ones failed to give convincing testimony, it was his intention to call only about five of the students to speak to the uproar over Lucy. He would then call Lucy and, after her, Dr Ring. After that he would have Alice and Caroline in the witness box; and he would finish off with Mary Campbell as the final most damning evidence against Miss Clegg.

'And now, ladies, if you will excuse me, I will snatch a bite to eat and then spend the rest of the evening rehearsing the questions I will be putting, and preparing my final summation to the Court. And Caroline, can I again remind you that tomorrow you are to be Miss Demure.'

Caroline said she would be as good as gold and the Burtons left James to his work. As they went outside, Alice commented that, while they were all exhausted by the day in Court, poor James was just embarking on a hard night's work. And Caroline enthusiastically agreed.

33

The next day in Court opened to the same noisy spectators in the public benches who only quietened down when the Court Usher led in the Judge. As he had explained, James began by leading evidence from the five students who, he had found in interviews, would give the strongest opinions. As instructed they allowed him to lead them at the beginning in praising Miss Clegg for her achievements both in her early career and in setting up the College and for being a role model for women's education. The contrast was all the more stark when they described her treatment of Lucy. They variously described her attack on Lucy as strident, malevolent, vicious and cruel. When asked, they said that Lucy had completely collapsed under the onslaught and that every girl in the class had come to her aid and protested to Miss Clegg about her treatment. They denied that either of the Burton sisters had formed a particularly leading role in the protest, which was fuelled by the popularity of Lucy and by the common belief that she had done nothing wrong.

They confirmed that it was only after emotions had calmed down a little that, acting on Mary Campbell's advice, they had agreed the wording of a letter to Miss Clegg which they hoped would have the effect of resolving the dispute.

James gave a little smile to Alice and Caroline to show he was pleased with the way the girls gave their evidence and he was equally happy that they stuck to their guns under cross-examination. He then called Lucy to the witness box. In the time it took Lucy to reach the witness box and to confirm her name to James the whole mood of the courtroom lightened. Lucy had so obviously such a lovely nature that, as Caroline had said when they first had met, you couldn't help but smile at her. Even the rather crotchety old Judge found himself unconsciously relaxing. She gave her evidence nervously but clearly and, in particular, confirmed that she took no part in her final certificate being granted.

She explained that she had felt sorry for Dr Ring and wanted to be as helpful to him as she could in preparing for his lectures and in clearing up afterwards. James allowed her to finish her narration of what had taken place and then turned to her with a stern face. 'You are a weak, deceitful liar whose underhand intrigues have brought disgrace on yourself and on The College for the Education and Promotion of Ladies in Medicine.'

There was an audible gasp in the Courtroom. Lucy almost staggered and her mouth fell open.

James turned to her again this time with a smile. 'That's just not true, is it Lucy?' He should have said Miss Dalrymple, but he could not help himself. 'I don't believe it for a second. Your classmates didn't believe it for a second. And, apart from one misguided person,' (looking with some contempt at Miss Clegg), 'no-one in this courtroom who has seen you believes it for a second. I have no further questions for this young lady who has been so grossly maligned.'

Miss Clegg's lawyer hesitated for a second but then, reading the feeling in the Courtroom, declined to cross-exam, allowing Lucy to leave the witness box to an outburst of applause from the public gallery, which the Court Usher hurriedly quelled.

The next witness was Dr Ring. (While questioning him, James had the greatest difficulty in not using his nickname Dr Boring because, in all his interviews with the students, this was the name which they used). As might be expected he spoke diffidently but his evidence was simple. He first knew of Lucy before he met her because it was with his help that she was permitted to start her course without having obtained the full certificate. Once he met her, he established an easy relationship with her and she often chatted about her background. It was through this that he learnt how much she missed her father who had died last year. Miss Dalrymple did not link this in any way with her examination performance, rather it was he who realised that the father's final illness and death had coincided with those examinations in which she had done less well than expected. He felt an injustice might have been done and approached the examining body on his own volition without telling her. Even when she thereafter told him that her full Certificate had come through he did not disclose his part in the affair. He had explained all this to Miss Clegg, but she refused to listen to him and virtually accused him of being in league with Lucy to bring pressure on the examiners.

James was happy with Dr Ring's evidence, but he was worried how he would stand up to rigorous cross-examination, which began by Miss Clegg's lawyer questioning him on his preparations for his job.

'Did Miss Clegg, knowing that you had no experience with female students, not warn you of the specific dangers of becoming too close to them?'

'It was scarcely necessary, but she did.'

'Despite this you allowed yourself to become a confident of Miss Dalrymple when you and she were alone together.'

Dr Ring flinched at that. If he were strictly honest with himself, he could have rebuffed her friendly approaches but his dried-up emotional being could not resist her open affectionate nature. It was like spring sunshine on an over-wintered plant although he could not have thought it in that way, far less express it so. But to James' delight the doctorBu responded more strongly than James had given him credit for.

'I take exception to the implications of your reference to us being alone together. Miss Dalrymple fell into the habit of assisting me in preparing my materials for my lectures and tidying up afterwards but, at all times, other students would be either drifting in for the lecture or drifting away afterwards. When doing so we naturally fell into conversation or rather Miss Dalrymple did as I am not a talkative person by nature.'

'And you are asking the Court to belief that you made the approach to the examiners without her encouragement, however subtle?'

'Yes'

'And when she told you that she had received her full Certificate you did not take the pleasure of disclosing your part in her success?'

'You will be familiar with the precept in Matthew Chapter 6.'

Miss Clegg's lawyer was flummoxed. He had no idea what Dr Ring was referring to and feared he might be exposed as not knowing what everyone else did. But years of court experience came to his aid.

'Perhaps you would elucidate for the benefit of the Court.'

The 'Court' was similarly at a loss but, in his turn, disliked the implication that only he was ignorant.

Dr Ring smiled, 'Your almsgiving must be secret and your Father who sees all that is done in secret will reward you.'

'Would you have been so generous if the recipient of your kindness had been a male student?'

'I was trying to right an injustice; anything else was irrelevant.'

Mr Annan tried a few more questions but Dr Ring held firm and was finally allowed to leave the witness box, much to his own relief and that of James.

Dr Ring was followed by Alice who told her story as previously narrated. In cross-examination, Mr Annan pressed Alice about the Hospital Incident, about which she repeated her regrets.

'Yes, Miss Burton, and the Hospital Superintendent, much to her credit, magnanimously played down the incident. And so, it is difficult at this length of time to gauge just how badly the persons involved behaved. Except for one piece of evidence. The Court has heard of the letter of apology which Miss Clegg prepared and which was signed voluntarily - and I emphasise **voluntarily** - by the four students who were involved.

'Miss Burton, you signed the letter, I believe.'

Alice nodded and tried to speak but was waved down by the lawyer.

'And with Miss Clegg's prompt action that was the end of the Incident - or should have been, and as such we would not be here discussing it. But no. You sent a further letter to Miss Murdoch without speaking first of all to Miss Clegg. Here is the letter. Perhaps you would read it to the Court.'

At this stage James rose to his feet to object, but the Judge over-ruled the objection and told Alice to read out the letter, which she did in a faltering voice.

"I wish to withdraw the apology sent to you yesterday. It was prepared by Miss Clegg and as soon as it was sent I regretted having signed it. I am sure that you find it as unpleasant to receive a forced apology as it was for me to sign it. I regret that our absorption in the treatment being given to the injured patient by the House Surgeon made us overlook the hospital regulations which are your province. I regret that this may have caused offence."

A murmur ran around the public benches at the terms of the letter, but the noise was quickly quelled by a stern look from the Court Usher. Mr Annan pressed her.

'That letter was sent behind Miss Clegg's back and was therefore deceitful.'

Alice answered in a firm voice. 'It was '

'And the terms of the letter are arrogant, are they not? And they are self-serving rather than apologetic, are they not?'

Again, Alice answered firmly. 'Yes. There were reasons but not excuses for what I did. I find it unpleasant to have my mistakes dissected in public just as we dissect specimens in the anatomy class. I regret what happened, but I was wrong. I admitted it then and I admit it now.'

James murmured under his breath, 'Good girl' especially as Mr Annan, despite Miss Clegg's frowning, then turned to the Certificate Incident where she denied the accusation that she was a ringleader and where he could not shake her from her statement that the reaction was not just hers but was the reaction of the entire class.

In re-examination, James asked her to explain what she meant when she said she had reasons for her action but not excuses. What were the reasons?

'Well, one only. I was passionate about wanting to study medicine and I was passionate about taking advantage of every opportunity to learn more. I felt that I was being deprived of this when Miss Murdoch intervened. I wonder if this is the difference between Miss Clegg and me. I was inspired initially by Miss Clegg but realised later that my sole motivation in taking up the study of medicine was the thought of helping the sick whereas Miss Clegg's concentration seemed to be on the advancement of women's education generally. I wonder whether this difference in emphasis was the cause of some of the undoubted friction between us.'

Miss Clegg was furious at this last statement and pulled at Mr Annan's gown to get him to refute it. His whispered explanation that it was not competent after re-examination, she dismissed as humbug.

When Caroline was being cross-examined the main aim of Mr Annan was to spark her into a show of that insubordination which he knew from Miss Clegg was there, but she stuck to the line of behaviour James had laid down. There was only one tricky moment when Miss Clegg's lawyer suggested to her that Mrs Black's opinion of her was that she was totally subversive and undisciplined. For a second Caroline's eyes glinted, and it crossed her mind to retort that only a fool would place any value on Mrs Black's opinion. However, she controlled herself and responded sweetly that she realised early in life that not everyone is going to like you. Alice marvelled at her sister's composure, so unlike the real Caroline, but she sustained it throughout her whole time in the box - much to Mrs Black's indignation.

And much to James's relief, the final witness was Margaret Campbell because it had been a draining day in Court for him and he was glad to be on the home stretch. As with the other students he led her through the initial praise for Miss Clegg and obtained her confirmation that she was possibly best placed to comment on her actions because she lodged with her.

'You were close to Miss Clegg?'

'I wouldn't say close. I know her better than the other students because I have the benefit of lodging with her.'

'Would you agree with me that Miss Clegg's conduct towards Miss Dalrymple on the day in question was totally out of order?'

'No, I would not agree with that at all. Miss Clegg did what she had to do.'

There were gasps around the Courtroom. Alice and Caroline gazed at Margaret in incredulity; James was completely flummoxed; even the Judge looked up from the notes he was taking and looked at Margaret over his glasses. Miss Clegg, who had sat through the succession of students giving evidence against her, suddenly took renewed interest.

James had no idea where he was going, but recovered himself sufficiently to say, 'I am sorry. You are now saying that Miss Clegg did nothing wrong in attacking Miss Dalrymple, an attack which your fellow students have described as vicious and malevolent?'

'In my view, Miss Clegg spoke strongly but nothing more. Miss Dalrymple is a lovely girl and a popular one, but she is vulnerable and when the students heard her being addressed in this way they naturally rallied to her aid. I did myself at the time, but I have more recently realised that just because someone is hurt that does not mean that the criticism is not justified.'

James, his mind still in a whirl as his clinching witness turned against him, said 'Have you always held these views?'

'No. I held a contrary view, but I changed my mind when I was sitting on my own in the witness room waiting to be called and I must apologise to you and to my friends for doing so; but I must do what I feel is right. Miss Clegg has always taught that if there are two options choose the harder one. A loving parent will often chastise a much-loved child. While I was waiting, I saw more clearly the problems Miss Clegg was fighting to overcome. For a woman to qualify as a doctor it is ten times harder than for a man and then ten times harder still. A man, who does not face these problems, cannot begin to appreciate the scale of the task. It requires self-discipline; it requires self-denial. It can mean the loss of friendships which is what I fear that I have done now. It may almost turn you into a non-woman. That may be the cost. But what Miss Clegg did, she did because she cares so much not just for the College but for all the students in it.'

James did not interrupt Margaret's statement because there was no convenient chance to intervene and in any event the length of her statement gave him time to regroup. 'Thank you, Miss Campbell. I bear no animus because you have changed your evidence and I am sure that the Pursuers will not either. You are under oath to tell the truth as you see it. But tell me this. At the time of the incident did you share in the general outcry following on Miss Clegg's words and the protests made?'

'Yes, I did.'

'Were the Pursuers leaders of this outcry or just part of the whole?'

'Just part of the general protest.'

'And so, no matter what your views are now, at the time you shared the view that Miss Clegg had behaved badly and that it was right to protest against her actings?'

'Yes. I am merely trying to justify why she had acted as she did.'

'But, although you were not in a position to hear her evidence, Miss Clegg has told this Court that she does not have to justify her decisions.'

'I cannot comment on that.'

James left the matter there having recovered the lost ground to his satisfaction and Mr Annan found himself in the position that, because of Margaret's change of heart, he did not require to cross-examine.

All that was left were was final summations by the respective lawyers.

34

Before Mr Annan could rise, James motioned to him and then rose, himself, to ask the Court if he could have a few moments to discuss certain matters further with his clients. When he was told that this would only take a few moments, the Judge said he would remain on the bench. While the Judge busied himself with checking his notes, James turned to speak to Alice and Caroline and with Mr Burton, who was seated in the front row of the public benches. This was all to the accompaniment of murmured speculation from the spectators, which the Court Usher chose to ignore. James told them that, in his view, while before the start of the Proof the question of reinstatement was in the balance, Margaret's evidence had changed things. He now had grave doubts as to whether the Court would grant that part of their petition seeking an Order that the Trustees should be compelled to re-admit the girls. To persist in this might imperil success in the more important part of the case. Given that alternative arrangements were available for the girls' continuing medical education, his recommendation was that they should drop that part of the case.

Caroline, alone, was all for fighting on but, in light of the combined opposition of the others, she agreed to accept James' recommendation. Thus, he rose to request the Court's permission to withdraw the plea for reinstatement, which was readily granted.

Mr Annan rose to address the Court. Before doing so, with Miss Clegg watching suspiciously, he leant across to James and whispered in his lugubrious way, 'You've taken away the best part of my remarks with that withdrawal.'

And this was true. The prospect of a Court trying to force someone to give instruction to another against their will offended all Mr Annan's sense of justice. He was prepared to speak passionately against such a possibility, hoping that the Court, in accepting his argument, might then be influenced to be with him on the remaining aspects of the case. But that part of the case having been removed, he was left to speak on the remaining matters, about which he could not summon up any passion whatsoever.

Mr Annan had often appeared for clients whom he did not admire but, in such cases, he was able to muster enthusiasm with the thought that it was his job to be the effective mouthpiece for those who were unable adequately to speak for themselves. But Miss Clegg had made it clear throughout the Proof, whether by pulling faces or by constant tugging at his gown when he was on his feet, that she felt herself more competent than he was, to conduct the Proof. Moreover, if truth be told, his sympathies lay all on the other side.

Because of this, although, in his remarks, he diligently covered all the relevant arguments in the case, he did so, to Miss Clegg's displeasure, without any persuasive force.

Meanwhile the Judge, as he had been throughout, was noting the demeanour of the respective parties as he took notes.

James, as he rose to address the Court, was very conscious that every eye in the courtroom was on him. He began by praising Miss Clegg for her achievements, saying that, in doing so, he was merely echoing the sentiments of every witness who had given evidence, (as might be expected, this merely evoked pursed lips from Miss Clegg). He went on,

'I do not intend to waste the Court's time over the Certificate Incident. The facts are not in dispute and, for the life of me, and I trust Your Lordship will agree, I cannot discern any fault whatsoever in my Clients' actions.

'The Hospital Incident is a different matter. There is no doubt that here there was fault. Miss Burton explained that the reason for her actions was an over enthusiasm for her chosen profession. To her credit, she accepted that that was no excuse.'

There was a just audible 'humph' from Miss Clegg at this point, which James acknowledged with a raised eyebrow but without comment.

'I repeat, there was fault. That she was in the wrong, Miss Burton accepted, and she apologised for it. When my learned friend made her read out in open court her ill-chosen words in that hasty letter, she faced up to that humiliation. Just as she had faced up to her admission of wrong at the time. What courage! What strength of character! What a person to have in your corner in a tight situation! Little wonder that her colleagues automatically looked up to her.

'The party chiefly offended, the Lady Superintendent, both in re-acting against the initial conduct and in accepted the apology with good grace, showed a dignity which reflected well why she had been chosen for her post. She thereafter worked without friction with Miss Burton, indeed, referring to her as an asset to the Infirmary.

' I suppose that one might expect that Mr Bryden, the Chairman of the Board of Trustees, as a man of the cloth, would extend forgiveness, but not all would have. He did. He accepted the apology and regarded the matter as closed.

'But one party did not regard the matter as closed. Like Tam O' Shanter's wife she nursed her wrath to keep it warm.' James paused slightly at this point to allow appreciation of his analogy of which he was quite proud. 'Miss Clegg carried forward her resentment and she subsequently allowed it to colour her whole attitude to my clients. She was on the look-out for every action which could be interpreted as a slight. Only she, with this preconceived prejudice, could fault my clients for their subsequent actions. Only Margaret Campbell, whose courage and honesty I applaud, attempted to defend Miss Clegg but she did so on the grounds of necessary discipline, which in my view trampled all over the decent treatment which my clients were entitled to expect.

'If, as I hope, your Lordship finds in favour of my clients I would ask your Lordship not only to order the reimbursement of the fees paid by my clients but, when deciding on the amount of additional damages to which my clients are entitled, to reflect on the numbers who have filled this Courtroom day after day. My clients' reputations throughout the city have been traduced by the actions of Miss Clegg. No monetary award can compensate for this, but the amount of the award will emphasise the wrong which was done to them.'

James sat down to a flutter of applause from the spectators' seats which was speedily silenced by the Court Usher rising to his feet with a frown on his face. The

Judge then adjourned the case to the following day when he would announce his verdict.

35

That night, awaiting the verdict, only Roddy got much sleep. That was not only because he was someone who enjoyed a good night's sleep but also because he was not as much involved as the others. He had attended the proof intermittently when his study commitments permitted but had no great feeling as to how it was progressing. He naturally hoped that the Burton sisters would be successful, but his main wish was that it would be all over so that he could again capture Caroline's attention; in the lead up to the proof and increasingly during it, she was preoccupied and had little time to devote to him.

Alice was downcast. She was flattered but embarrassed by James' description of her in his summing-up. She was saddened to feel that the whole noble enterprise on which they had embarked just over a year earlier had descended to such an ignoble end. And despite everything she still retained the greatest respect for Miss Clegg's achievements. She had not seen a lion being hounded by a pack of hyenas nor a bull nearing its end in the bullring, but she had read about such things and, as she watched James in court goading Miss Clegg, she felt that she also was like some proud animal at bay. Whatever the outcome, no-one was going to win tomorrow.

Caroline was too excited to sleep. Once the proceedings against Miss Clegg had been issued, thinking about the case had occupied much of her waking hours and, once the proof had started she had delighted in the cut and thrust of the legal process. She was nervous leading up to giving her own evidence but felt she had comported herself reasonably well. She felt that she had acted with all the decorum of one of Jane Austen's heroines. Once that was over she had relished the skilful way in which James Morrison had teased out the evidence from witnesses.

'I would be good at that,' she thought. 'I could be like Portia in The Merchant of Venice leading on the witness into a trap. I would love to do that' But she knew that there was an infinitely less chance of her pursuing a legal career than there was in her qualifying as a doctor. As she eventually did drift off to sleep her last dreamy thought was of James Morrison. She thought he had looked very handsome in his legal gown.

Mrs Black lay thinking back over the evidence she had given. Had she done enough to help Miss Clegg against those vicious sisters? Was there anything else she could have said? She thought back to how much she owed Miss Clegg. In her earlier married life, it was to Miss Clegg she had turned when her husband and her two young children had fallen ill during that terrible epidemic. Mrs Black, of course, could not afford a doctor and it was one of her neighbours who told her that there was a lady doctor who was always prepared to give treatment, taking as payment only what the patients could afford. Through those dark December days Miss Clegg was assiduous in her attendance, although there was little she could do apart from making the poor patients as comfortable as possible.

None of them survived; her infant son was the last entry in the Register of Deaths that December, her husband and her three-year old daughter the first two entries of the following year. After the deaths, Mrs Black, who too, had suffered from the outbreak, was slowly recovering and Miss Clegg continued to call to enquire after her well- being. Quite apart from the state of Mrs Black's health there was the problem of keeping on the house and, at that stage, she had no source of income. Then, in the course of one visit, Miss Clegg suggested to Mrs Black that she might like to come and work for her in her house. Mrs Black jumped at the chance. She gave Miss Clegg devoted service working firstly as a maid and thereafter, as Miss Clegg realised that, despite her lack of education, she was a highly intelligent woman, as a general assistant.

Mrs Black felt that only she knew the real Miss Clegg. The reality was that Miss Clegg, without meaning to, had built a wall round herself against all comers. When someone smiles, it is like an invitation; Miss Clegg's smile never left the front of her face. It is only when she was dealing with someone who was helpless and posed no threat, such as a seriously ill person, that the defences come down and she allowed herself to run the risk of exposing her own vulnerability.

That night Miss Clegg felt vulnerable, indeed. She shuddered as she thought back to what had happened in Court. Outrageous, the depiction of Alice Burton as some sort of heroine. And how did that man know anything about Mary Jane? Of course, it was public knowledge that Mary Jane had died, but there had never been a public suggestion that her death was in any way Miss Clegg's responsibility. It was only Miss Clegg who, in her heart, had blamed herself for driving Mary Jane so hard and for not seeing, in one who was so close, the tell-tale signs of decline. She could have saved her, she was sure, had she not been so blinded by her determination to further the cause.

Mary Jane had shared her ambitions but not her strength and Miss Clegg had allowed someone to suffer whom she had ... **No**. She couldn't allow herself even, in the recesses of her mind, to use the word. Someone for whom she had the greatest affection.

The little box that lay on her desk was a present from Mary Jane. It was the only gift that Miss Clegg had ever received in an adult life during which she herself had never given one. In her first despair, when Mary Jane had died, Miss Clegg had often wanted to throw it away, but something always held her back and it remained there on her desk, something for which she unconsciously reached to stroke in moments of stress

In a locked drawer in her desk Miss Clegg kept the last letter which Mary Jane had sent her. She didn't need to take it out to read it. She knew it off by heart.

'Dear Jennifer,

I fear that your little friend has not much left in her. I have been privileged to work with you over the past years and I am only sorry that I could contribute so little. You have borne my inadequacies with such patience. It has been the happiest time of my life living with you and I have no regrets. I leave no legacy but maybe you will retain a place in your heart for someone who loved you dearly and use that as a spur to drive you to even greater efforts for the cause which we both cherished.

I'm sorry but I am too weak to write any more. Typical of me.
With all my love,

Mary Jane'

Miss Clegg always fought against thinking of that letter because whenever she did she felt as if she was being stabbed in the heart. She struggled against these thoughts now and gradually, although the physical pain was still there, she recovered control of her feelings and directed her mind to the verdict tomorrow. She was still indignant about the performance of Mr Annan. Mr Anon, more like, for all the good he was. She had no qualms about what she had done with regard to the Burton sisters. She had had no alternative if she were to retain control of her College. Whether the Judge with the to-be-expected male prejudice would agree was another matter. She steeled herself for whatever might be the outcome.

Margaret had a troubled night. At the end of the proof Caroline had walked right past her without saying a word but Alice had approached her and shook her hand and assured her that she bore no ill-will against her. Margaret went over in her mind endlessly, the events of the day. Before she left for the Court that morning she had received a letter from the two Dunlop sisters in the village who had done so much to enable her to enter the College. They hoped she was well and would be able to give continuing support to Miss Clegg. Then as she sat nervously in the witness room there came the sudden realisation that, if the sisters won their case, that would be the end of the College and of her own ambitions. There was no possibility of Miss Clegg taking the sisters back, but the sisters were from a rich family. If the College closed, they would no doubt be able to pursue a medical career abroad if they wished, or to follow some other interests. But what would come of her with her poor background, with the hopes of her old friends in the village dashed.

As she lay in the dark she tortured herself with the thought that she might have allowed her own self-interest to influence what she had done, but she was clear on one thing. At the moment when she suddenly decided to change her testimony, something in her had also changed. She was no longer a mere assistant to Miss Clegg, she had become a sister with her in the fight Despite this it was only many years later, when she had qualified as a doctor, following in the rigorous steps of Miss Clegg, that she was able to be totally happy within herself that she had done the right thing.

36

'Court'

With this word the Court Usher brought the whole courtroom to its feet, to greet the entrance of the Judge. There was a rustle of silks as the predominantly female spectators rose and then, as they now knew to do, bowed to the judge before resuming their seats. The room was packed to overflowing; a queue had formed outside before the Court opened and some had even sent their maids to try to reserve a place in it. Choices of clothes had been made as if this was the first night at the opera. Looking down from his perch the venerable Judge had never seen such a riot of colour. He was not sure that he approved of his Court becoming a public spectacle – but he liked the audience. There was a murmur of anticipation as the Judge sorted his papers which died away as he started to speak.

'The Defenders in this case are the Trustees of the College for the Education and Promotion of Ladies in Medicine. The Pursuers are Miss Alice Burton and Miss Caroline Burton. Both parties agree that there was a contract between the parties whereby the Defenders undertook to provide for the Pursuers a four-year course of medical instruction which would prepare the Pursuers to take the examinations set by one of the approved medical societies to become a medical practitioner. What the Court is asked to determine is whether, because of the actions of the Pursuers, the Defenders are entitled to cancel this contract or whether the Defenders are in breach of it.

'The Pursuers originally sought not only damages for breach but also performance of the remaining years of the contract. I must confess that, whatever my decision on the merits, I would have had difficulty, given the breakdown of the relationship between the parties, in giving an order compelling performance. However, prior to his final summation Mr Morrison for the Pursuers intimated the withdrawal of that part of their claim and this was accepted by the Defenders.

'Although the named Trustees are correctly named as Defenders it is clear that they took little or no part in the events which took place and the main protagonist is really Miss Jennifer Clegg who bears the title of Dean, possibly a slightly ambitious one for such a small organisation.

'The evidence given by witnesses was clear, and on the whole impartial. I would exclude in this context much of the evidence given by Mrs Black, who is described as Miss Clegg's secretary. It is clear that, from the very start, she developed a dislike of both of the Pursuers, and her evidence, possibly through a praiseworthy sense of loyalty to Miss Clegg, was slanted to put the Pursuers in a bad light. She described the Pursuers shrugging shoulders and looking at each other whenever she passed on Miss Clegg's instructions. When pressed as to what the Pursuers actually said, she replied that a woman can do a great deal by a look or a toss of the head or a whisper. That is as maybe, but I fear that the witness has fallen into the trap of recreating events mentally and then believing her version.

'That there were areas of conflict, I have no doubt, but no more than might be expected in a comparatively small group working together in a confined space. Miss Clegg's authoritarian concept of her position may have contributed to this. But I think also that there may have been a genuine difference in ideas. This was brought out by Miss Alice Burton in her evidence. She spoke movingly that her sole motive in embarking on medical training was to look after the sick and injured. However, she realised quite early on, when she looked back at how she had originally been so inspired by Miss Clegg's address at the opening of the session, that, in that address, Miss Clegg had not once mentioned the patients with whom they were going to work. And subsequently she realised that, whereas her only concern was to qualify as a doctor, Miss Clegg's main emphasis was on the general advancement of women, not particularly in medicine.

'In her evidence, Miss Clegg characterised Miss Alice Burton as the ringleader. This suggests a conspiracy or organised campaign which in my view did not exist. As Mr Morrison stated in his remarks, it would seem that, in the group of students, Miss Burton, without seeking it, emerged as a natural leader. Thereafter she became the spokesperson for the students' various complaints, but I heard no evidence that she was the fomenter of these complaints.'

As the Judge paused to turn a new page and adjust his spectacles there was a quiet murmur from the spectator benches but not enough to warrant any action from the Court Usher. The Judge continued in his quiet emotionless voice,

'The day to day discontents were, in my view, comparatively trivial and would never have led the parties to be in court. There were, however two major incidents which were important and regarded by the parties as such. The first was what became known as the Hospital Incident. For their part in this the Pursuers were completely in the wrong. At their whim, they broke a clear rule of the College and indeed of the hospital: when reprimanded by the Lady Superintendent they disputed her authority; they compounded their offence in some high-handed exchange of letters with her; they argued with Miss Clegg about what had happened and what should be done. This was wrong. However, what exacerbated the situation was Miss Clegg's way of dealing with it.

'For the Pursuers, the rule was just one of the many petty restrictions which Miss Clegg imposed on her students without explanation and which all the students, not just the Pursuers, found irksome and unnecessary. However, this particular rule, although laid down by Miss Clegg, was imposed by the hospital authorities and Miss Clegg had a real fear that the privilege of access to the hospital would be withdrawn leaving the College unable to continue teaching medicine. Had she communicated this to the students, who have all struck me as intelligent responsible young ladies, I have no doubt they would have reacted accordingly. But she did not. When pressed on this in cross-examination, she stated that it was not her habit to explain her motives to students. Moreover, she chose to deal with the matter by way of public rebuke before the assembled students. This, I think was unwise.'

This time there was a discernible hubbub from the spectators, which the Court Usher quelled with a frown.

'Be that as it may, following the initial row the affected students accepted a two-week suspension of privileges and matters settled down again. The Lady

Superintendent accepted the final apologies and she confirmed in evidence that what she regarded as an unpleasant affair was at an end. Thereafter the five o'clock rule was punctually observed, and she had no subsequent complaints about the conduct of the students. Indeed, she spoke in a complimentary fashion about her subsequent relationship with Miss Alice Burton.

'Had matters finished there the Chairman of the Trustees, when asked, confirmed that no further action would have been taken against the Pursuers and we would not be in court today. Accordingly, we must now turn to the second major incident, the controversy over Miss Lucy Dalrymple's Certificate.'

As the Judge once more paused, the Court Usher was alert for any sign of what he might regard as inappropriate behaviour, but the audience were too absorbed in the Judge's words to move or say anything.

'It is clear from the evidence both of Miss Dalrymple and Dr Ring that Miss Dalrymple had no part in the examiners being requested to re-consider her papers in light of her personal circumstances at the time of sitting the examination. The issuing of the Certificate should have been a matter of satisfaction to Miss Clegg because after all it had been partly through her efforts that Miss Dalrymple had been permitted to embark on her course of medical instruction without the Certificate first having been obtained. But for reasons which I do not understand, Miss Clegg felt bound to interfere. What she had to do with it I do not know. She took the trouble of cross-examining Miss Dalrymple but disbelieved or refused to accept her explanation. She then communicated with Dr Ring and seems to have doubted or disbelieved even him.

'Subsequent to this, in an open meeting with all the students, the evidence is that she harangued Miss Dalrymple and made a violent attack on her conduct characterising it as mean and dishonourable. In her evidence, Miss Clegg attempted to play down the strength of her attack but the evidence of numerous of the students was that it was vituperative and indeed reduced Miss Dalrymple to tears. It was only to be expected that the other ladies, not just the Pursuers, resented the accusations and that the argument that followed became extremely heated. The only differing voice in the evidence of all the students was that of Miss Margaret Campbell who was called as a witness for the Pursuers but had clearly changed her view. She was a perfectly sound witness and was quite entitled to her change of opinion but the evidence she gave formed a reason for Miss Clegg's actions and not an excuse for them.

'It was to be expected that following the upheaval there was a continuing unpleasant atmosphere throughout the College. Thereafter Miss Clegg presented an ultimatum to the Board of Trustees; either the Pursuers should go, or she would go.

'I should make it clear that Miss Clegg' achievements are considerable and command our admiration; all the young ladies, even those whom she had apparently injured, conceded this in giving evidence. No doubt, in the course of dealing with her, they sometimes forgot, under the provocation of her masterful ways, how much they were indebted to her and to her efforts. But it would seem that, from the outset, Miss Clegg had an exaggerated view of her position and of her powers and by demanding too much received less than she was entitled to. Certainly, when it came to the dismissal of the Pursuers she was of the opinion, from which the Trustees could not shake her, that she was entitled to terminate their course of education willy-nilly.'

Throughout the Judge's reading Miss Clegg frowned from time to time to show her displeasure at what he was saying, but, at this point, she vigorously shook her head in disagreement.

The Judge continued, 'I do not share the view that the contract between the Pursuers and the Defenders was one which the Defenders were entitled to terminate at their whim. Nor do I think that the conduct of the Pursuers as brought out in evidence was sufficiently injurious to justify the termination, on the basis of their conduct. I therefore find for the Pursuers and award in their favour a monetary sum. This will be calculated by the Clerk to the Court to compensate them for the academic fees paid of which they have received no benefit, with an amount, which I assess at four times the amount of these fees, to reflect the wrong they have suffered. In the nature of things, I also award expenses of the Action to the Pursuers.'

As the Judge finished speaking there was outburst of applause from the public benches which sustained, despite the Court Usher's best efforts, until the Judge rose and left the Courtroom, when it redoubled in volume.

Throughout the judge's delivery of his opinion, Miss Clegg had sat motionless, her back as usual not touching the back of the bench. Although she had her counsel and Mrs Black beside her she seemed a solitary detached figure. An onlooker, watching her as the Judge spoke, could have read her disquiet; she had a sense of foreboding as soon as the judge made the disparaging comment about her title of Dean. As he went on she realised that he had totally failed to appreciate the magnitude of the task which had faced her, and which had demanded her total control.

At the mention of the admiration to which she was due her spirits were raised a little, but they were immediately dashed by his totally false description of the relations between her and her students. The final outcome was accordingly expected but still a blow when it came. She was indignant when Mr Annan leant over to extend a bony hand to shake with James Morrison.

She was later to reflect that the judgement was just another example of male authority preening itself for protecting the weaker sex against attack, even though in this case it was feminine strength which was the perceived attacker. She had no doubt that had the Pursuers been men they would not have won the case. But now when the Judge left the courtroom she turned to Margaret Campbell who was sitting behind her. 'Thank you, Margaret,' she said. She then rose to her feet, ignoring Mr Annan and marched out of the room without saying another word, with head held high, looking neither to left or right, but with Margaret Campbell at her side, and Mrs Black bobbing in her wake. The fight would go on.

The reaction on the other side of the courtroom was totally different. As soon as the judge left there was considerable noise and bustle as the girls hugged each other and their supporters, while behind them in the public benches the spectators, who had been listening spellbound, rose to their feet to applaud the result. Some left right away so as to be the first to spread the news. Others, including some who would have been glad to see the sisters brought down a peg, crowded round them to offer their congratulations.

Mr Burton, who had sat throughout the whole three days of evidence, slapped the desk in front of him in triumph before leaning forward to shake hands with James.

Alice also shook his hand and expressed her thanks. Caroline, however, abandoning the Jane Austen mode she had adopted for the Proof, turned to him and, without speaking, gave him an enthusiastic kiss on the cheek.

Once things had quietened down somewhat, Mr Burton left the girls to their celebrations. His job was done but, as a loner accustomed to ploughing a lonely furrow, he had no friends to share the triumph with. He set off home to share it with those to whom it meant the most, his wife and Anna.

Meanwhile, Caroline linked her arm in James's and, arm in arm, they led their supporters in procession from the courthouse like a happy couple emerging from church after their wedding.

Roddy was outside watching from a distance. He deduced from the noisy reactions of those who emerged that the sisters had won. He saw Caroline come out, smiling up at James. Then he turned up his coat collar and trudged back up the hill to the hospital.

Epilogue

Miss Clegg continued with her College and with her general work for the advancement of women. In this she was aided by Margaret Campbell who qualified as a medical practitioner and eventually took over Miss Clegg's role as a leader of the movement.

Lucy Dalrymple did not finish her course but two of her daughters subsequently accomplished what her mother had failed to do and qualified as doctors.

Alice Burton qualified as a doctor and, after practising for a number of years, married Roddy MacDonald who became a leading figure in medical research and was knighted for his work.

Caroline did become a medical missionary and spent her entire working life in West Africa where she died. She never married.

Printed in Great Britain
by Amazon